GONE BUT NOT MISSED

A NATHAN MICCOLI MYSTERY

A R Kennedy

Copyright © 2013 A R Kennedy
All rights reserved.

ISBN: 1493500937
ISBN13: 9781493500932

TO H & L
the inspiration for Laude

TO MY BETA READERS
Jackie, Mom, Gina, Jodi & Phil

LILY

Saturday February 14, 2009

I woke with a terrible headache. The pounding reminded me of the night Annie and I discovered the potency and, the next morning, the after effects of martinis. The smile that thought brought to my face quickly faded when the throbbing intensified.

I feared opening my eyes. Not sure if that would make my head hurt worse and scared what I would see. I tried to recall my evening. I didn't remember going to bed. Truth was, I didn't remember coming home.

No. I remembered getting on the elevator. And, arguing on the phone with Annie, before getting on the elevator. And hanging up on Annie as I got on the elevator. But that was it. No getting into my apartment; no getting into my bed. I was trying to remember more when I remembered the most important thing, Laude.

I gradually opened my eyes and there she was. Sitting right next to me, staring at me. Her ears, which usually stood straight up, were down. Her head was down, too. Not exactly cowering but not the usual morning, happy to see you posture of my puppy. It was a bit disconcerting to see those two dark eyes fixed on me, never mind not knowing how long they had been staring at me.

It was strange she hadn't asked to go out yet. On weekday mornings, the alarm went off so early that neither of us were awake. On weekend mornings, I usually awoke to a paw tapping my arm and little yips if her initial attempts did not get me up.

I rolled over slowly, hoping slow movements would not increase the pain in my head, to see what time it was. The clock glowed '9:30', much later than our usual six in the morning wake up.

Something seemed off but I couldn't tell what it was. I quickly surveyed the room. Nightstand, dresser, pictures, everything looked fine. Except the shade was down; no wonder I had slept so late. The ocean sounded strong today, too. The waves, a block away, crashed on the shore louder than usual. Remembering the weather forecast, it must be from the impending storm.

"Time to go, Laude," I said. But she didn't move. I rolled out of bed and my feet felt the cushion of the carpet. Especially on cold mornings like this, I was glad Aunt Florence had chosen carpet instead of hardwood floors in the bedroom. The carpet felt even cushier this morning.

I looked down at my pajamas. They were my least favorite set, blue flannel, buttoned down the front and long sleeved. I always felt too warm to sleep in them. I didn't feel warm now though. I thought I had put the pajamas in the laundry earlier in the week but they looked clean, and even pressed—I didn't even own an iron. Annie would attest to that.

"It's potty time, Laude." She just sat there on the bed, staring at me.

"You feeling alright? Don't worry, the vet appointment will be just fine. If we leave now we can just make it." She couldn't possibly know she had a veterinarian appointment today. She may have become my constant companion over the past eight months but she was still a dog with a limited vocabulary, despite the amount I spoke to her.

I decided I would get dressed and even brush my hair. "Never know if there'll be a cute vet, right Laude?" I'd been listening to

Annie too much. I smiled at the thought. I had to call her. Hopefully she wasn't too mad about me hanging up on her. I was surprised she hadn't called me yet. I looked around the room and couldn't locate my cell phone.

I walked over to the window to raise the shade to let in the sun and to look at the ocean. But, the ocean wasn't there.

LILY

Sunday   5 p.m.   January 25, 2009   Long Beach, NY

"Did you get on yet?"
"Get on what?"
"You know."
"No, you'll have to tell me."
"Your birthday present."
"What? My birthday present. Oh my God, Annie, you shouldn't have! You didn't tell me you got me a pony. I've always wanted one." I said it with the smallest hint of sarcasm. She wasn't going to be amused.

"Lillian, I am not amused." I knew it. Of course, I misjudged just how much it wouldn't amuse her. I could tell how much something aggravated her by how much of my name she used. She spoke to her one year old son, my godson, Harold Brian Follette, the same way.

I could picture her on the other side of the phone. Standing in her large kitchen with its bay window looking out on their backyard, her hands clenched and her head shaking back and forth in frustration. I could hear Harry babbling in the background.

"What would you do with a pony anyway? I got you a much more practical gift and as we all know, your birthday was weeks ago."

"I don't think we all know. I'm still waiting for them to go around collecting the four dollars at work and get me a thoughtless gift card."

"Lily, I wouldn't hold my breath on that one." She settled down quickly, too bad. I could hear her return to cooking dinner while Harry played and cooed in the background. It's sad when the most entertaining part of your day is seeing how badly you can irritate your best friend.

Returning to thoughts of the pony, "Damn, I could've bought a nice riding outfit for it." We both laughed at the thought of that. The tall riding boots on my petite frame was the least of it. The thought of the riding hat over my unmanageable brown curly hair was very comical. Annie would have looked perfect in a riding outfit. It would have only accentuated her thin frame and good posture. Her straight brown hair, usually pulled back into a pony tail that hung to her mid-back, would not have fought wearing a riding hat.

Perfect would be the most apt way to describe her. Annie was a perfect mother and wife, living in a perfect four bedroom home in the suburbs of Philadelphia. She was also a perfect friend. Correction, She was until seven months ago.

Suppressing further laughter, Annie said, "There is no pony. And fortunately, for all, no riding outfit. Let it go."

"And what do you mean, 'What would I do with a pony?' We both know my equestrian aspirations." I tried my best to get that out without laughing. I succeeded but it was difficult.

"Yes, not falling off and breaking your ass." Annie was right, that would be the highest goal I could achieve with horseback riding. My dad used to say the same thing when I begged him as an eight year old to take me to the local riding center. Fortunately for him, my desire to horseback ride had lasted only a year, probably not even that long.

"Hope Harry didn't hear that," I told her.

"Don't worry, he heard far worse during your last visit." I did not agree but she was pretty steamed the first time she heard her precious one year old say "shit." She was "Genevieve Lillian Brannon" mad when he said it the tenth time, on the phone with her mother. Her husband, Jeffrey, and I had to leave the room so she wouldn't see or hear our laughter.

Interrupting my nice memory, she brought me back to the undesirable present. "Anyway, you only have to get started on your 'Journey to Love.'"

I'll never know what possessed her to get me a gift certificate for a dating site, never mind one so poorly named. The jingle from their commercial would be in my head the rest of the day. Some days I even caught myself singing it in the apartment.

I looked down at Laude who was looking up at me. I wasn't sure what she wanted. I did know what I wanted, out of this conversation.

"Gotta go. Laude has to potty."

"She seems to have to go a lot lately."

"Yep, talk to you later."

I knew Laude's bladder wouldn't always be able to get me off the phone with Annie. We both knew what it meant, and it was far less rude than hanging up on her, something I had never done. Funny thing is, whenever she said Harry had to potty, or more accurately, needed a diaper change, I always believed her.

Once Laude heard "potty", she was running to the door, tail wagging as fast as it could. I grabbed her leash and opened the door. She ran for the stairs. Laude stopped halfway to the stairwell and started barking at Ms. June, who was standing five feet away.

Mrs. June Roberto was the oldest resident of the building and was quick to tell everyone this at the bi-annual board meetings. She wasn't the president of the condo board but tried her best to run those meetings. The real president, Ronnie Herschowitz, did his best to listen to the oldest resident (in years in the building and years on the planet) and get her to sit back down. It was the only reason I attended those meetings. Even before I was an official resident, Aunt Florence would bring me for the comic relief.

"Sorry, Ms. June. I'll get her."

"That's alright. How are you today, Laude?" Looking down at Laude, she reached into her pocket. Laude knew what was coming and sat down, as best she could with her little tail now going double time. "She's always such a good girl." She patted Laude on the top of her head, gave her the treat, and headed for her apartment, two doors down from mine.

For an 88 year old widow, she was spry. With her neatly coiffed hair, still as dark brown as I remembered it twenty years ago, she walked the five mile boardwalk daily, even in the rain. She seemed to never forget a name or a face and would wave to her fellow walkers, runners, and bikers as she strided in her vibrantly colored lounge wear outfits. I think she had one in every color. I also thought she was in better shape than some of the forty year olds I worked with.

"Thank you, Ms. June." Laude sat contentedly, having finished the treat and I put her pink floral leash on.

"You're welcome. Have a nice day, Laude."

I'm not sure if she thought Laude spoke to her and she was replying. "A good girl" would be polite and thank her for the treat, right? Or, that she thought my name was Laude, too.

I wish I could say Ms. June was the exception. Laude and I had been living here six months. I had been visiting for over 23 years, lots of weekends and most of the summers. I didn't think anyone knew my name. That was an exaggeration. The super, Tony, knew it but that was only because he wanted a tip. And I seemed to call him a lot more than the other residents.

For starters, there was the incident in the shower that I didn't want to think about. I really didn't think a 60 year old man could move that fast. If he was younger, or if I was older, he might think I was intentionally doing things so I could have an excuse to have him in the apartment. The shower incident would have solidified it. In my defense, he said he would come in the afternoon to fix the door. To me, ten in the morning was not the afternoon.

When I told Annie about him walking into the apartment when I was in the shower, her first question was "Is he single?". She was disappointed when I answered he was over sixty. She replied "Well, too bad you didn't shock him enough to call 911. The police and fire departments have some good looking single men on them."

She was always looking for a way to pair me up. At first it was endearing, now it was just annoying.

During our ten minute walk, Laude got five "Hello, Laude's" and I did not get one "Hello, Lillian" or at worst "Genevieve." I'm not jealous. Well, alright, just a little. She is awful cute. And has far fewer bad hair days than me.

Back in the apartment, after removing Laude's leash, I got her a treat.

"How come you sit for Ms. June? I feed you, walk you and you never sit when I give you a treat." I swear she looked at me like Annie did when I visited last - with very little patience. Laude's un-cropped ears stood straight up and she tilted her head to the side. She was too cute to reprimand. I handed her the treat and she ran off to her bed to eat it. When she finished, she ran back with her favorite toy, a purple octopus. I could hear its squeaker as she ran back to me in anticipation of play. Instead, she dropped it to the floor as well as herself as I got out her hairbrush for her weekly brushing.

She had the proper miniature schnauzer haircut, closely trimmed back, neck, ears, throat and chest. Her eyebrows and beard were long, as well as the hair on her belly and legs. I had learned the hard way the importance of regular brushing. Her first haircut was a full body shave to remove the knots in her hair that left her looking pathetically skinny and not pretty. Annie told me I was more emotional about Laude's first haircut than she was about Harry's.

The phone rang as I finished Laude's brushing and it could only be one person- Annie. I prayed it was a telemarketer instead. Either way, the machine could get this one.

"I know you're already back from walking Laude. Now, get online and fill out the questionnaires and start your journey to love!" The sad part was that she believed this and, worse, that I was going to listen to her and answer all those inane questions. To be perfectly honest, I was surprised she hadn't filled out the questionnaire for me already. She seemed to think she knew me best and what was best for me.

She would say that she was so happy with her baby and husband. She just wanted me to have the same. In college, late at night, we would talk about the future. She already had marriage with Jeffrey on her mind. She was less pushy then about me finding a date.

After four years as roommates, she got what she wanted and soon thereafter left to get married and then had Harry. I stayed to finish my physical therapy degree. I was not sure when she went from roommate to sister but I could tell you when she went from sister to overbearing mother - when the spot came open.

LILY

Monday   6:00 am   January 26, 2009

"Good morning. It's Mike and Mike and we're back and better than ever," the radio blared.

I wished I could say the same. I also wished they would not start my day off poorly with more bad news regarding my beleaguered team. The last season had ended so poorly, a little bit of me was glad Dad hadn't seen it. It was his fault I thought spring started in mid-February - the day pitchers and catchers report. My mother blamed him too. Instead of playing with dolls, I played catch. Instead of Saturday tea parties, I went to Shea with Dad to see the New York Mets play. Mom did not love having to learn the score before we came home so she would know our moods.

I turned off the alarm before Mike or Mike proceeded. It would probably only be Super Bowl information today but better to be safe than sorry.

I turned over to see Laude, wide awake, stretching in her perfect downward dog pose. "Come on Laude, time to go." It was morning walk time. Fortunately, we don't run into too many people on our morning walks. Annie was not fond of my morning routine- first thing walk Laude.

"You know this is why you don't have a boyfriend. Who wants to date a girl who looks like that?" Although that sounds harsh, it was the truth. I tried to explain to her that a nine month old miniature schnauzer's bladder did not have the time or patience for me to get all dolled up. I didn't even go to the bathroom before her walk.

"Can you at least brush your hair?," she'd ask. Usually, I didn't remember that piece of advice until I had run into a cute jogger.

Laude had her post-breakfast treat and she made herself comfortable in her bed. In her eyes, I had no other purpose until dinner. "Have a nice day, Laude. Susie will be here later."

Susie was the dog walker. Laude met most of the neighbors with her. She left me notes everyday telling me about their time together- who they met, what treats she gave her, and more information about Laude's bowel and bladder routine than I cared to know. Worse was when the messages were more detailed. Not exactly pre-dinner reading material.

After twenty minutes of driving, I was at work and ready for my 7:30 patients. I was always amazed how busy I was at 7:30 in the morning. I knew the morning was going to go fast when I saw three people waiting in the lobby. Then I saw Alexa coming and I knew it wouldn't go fast enough.

She worked in the front office of the outpatient therapy facility. Usually you heard Alexa coming before you saw her, either her voice or the four inch heels she always wore would announce her intrusive arrival. Worst, she called me 'Jen.'

"Jen, I need four dollars for the birthday fund."

"Good morning, Alexa," I emphasized her lack of greeting. "Who's birthday?" I immediately regretted asking. It was not a big office but it seemed like one of the front desk personnel, all ladies, were always having a birthday. I didn't care about the four dollars but I could do without everyone being dragged into the office and singing "Happy Birthday." I did like the cake.

"One of the PTs, I don't know which one she is. She must work in one of the other offices. Usually Joan does all the birthday stuff for the clinical staff- collects the money, buys the gift, gets the cake, whatever. But, she must have forgot Genevieve's birthday. It was a couple weeks ago. Maybe she just doesn't like her. I don't know. All I know is Rosa felt bad for her and said she'd take care of it but sticks me with getting all the money." Looking aggravated, she put her hand out.

Part of me wanted to point out that I was Genevieve. I grabbed my purse and gave her the money instead. Nothing to worry about, I'd be getting it back.

I returned to my patients and the morning flew by. I had forgotten about the incident until Alexa came back to ask James for money. Good luck with that. I watched for my own amusement- would he roll his eyes, yell at her to leave him alone, tell her in his condescending tone how he had better things to do than talk to her about birthdays. If she thought Joan didn't like "Genevieve", wait until she talked to James.

I wasn't sure which was worse, the fact that they forgot my birthday or that weeks afterwards I was going to have to pretend to be happy and surprised when I was brought into the front office under a false, and most likely, lame pretense.

LILY

Tuesday   11:00 a.m.   January 27, 2009

I heard the intercom squawk and then Rosa's overly cheery voice. "Hey, Gen can you come up front and decipher your handwriting for me?"

"Can I do it later, Rosa? I'm a little busy right now." With two patients expectantly looking at me for their next exercise, I didn't think now was a good time to leave.

"No, I have to get the claim out today, so I need you up here now." I couldn't imagine what could be that urgent plus my handwriting was good. Usually if there was a problem, they brought the paperwork to me. Then it dawned on me that I had better put on my happy face and get this humiliation over as fast as possible. At least there would be cake.

I walked up front and prepared to act surprised. When I entered the office, the ladies stood around a boxed coffee cake with a lit match stuck in it. I didn't have to act. No candle, no bakery cake, no chocolate. Putting on a happy face was harder than I expected. At least, Alexa wasn't there and I wouldn't have to explain how I was Genevieve and not Jennifer.

If it wasn't so ridiculous I'd cry. But I forced a smile, blew out the "candle" and explained how I'd better get back to work. Looking back, I should have worded my wish better than "Get me out of here."

My pre-dinner routine started as usual with talking to Annie.

"How was your day?" Annie used to ask this lightly. While she was pregnant and I was interning, she asked hoping I would tell her a funny story about something a patient did or something that happened to me. She used to say it was the funniest part of her day. If she was having a bad day, she knew I would give her a good laugh and the stress would vanish. Often trying to suppress a giggle, unsuccessfully, she'd say "I'm glad I'm not you." No one else told her stories about getting locked in a storage closet or about a 90 year old grabbing their fanny. Now, she asked like she was afraid of what I was going to say. I could not decide if I was excited or embarrassed to tell her about my day.

"It was my birthday."

I expected a laugh, or to be told no it wasn't. I got, "Speaking of your birthday..."

Before she could finish that sentence, I interrupted, "Don't you want to know about my gift?"

"Where's the gift card for?," she answered. The six months I had worked at the outpatient physical center we had had eight birthdays and eight different gift cards, thoughtfully picked based on the recipients likes, hobbies, etc. I think we both thought the office would go with the obvious, The Mets Store, a couple miles from the office.

"A grocery store."

"Wow. A gift card is a pretty thoughtless gift but one for milk and bread makes it even worse. You'll be able to stock up on peanut butter and jelly." She sighed, "I have no idea how you eat a PB and J every day." In college, my propensity to eat a peanut butter and jelly sandwish was fine. As an adult, she found it peculiar and annoying. "Well, at least there was cake."

"I don't want to talk about it." I didn't want to discuss the matchmaking site either. "How was your day?," I asked, hoping this would get her on a twenty minute tangent while the water boiled for my pasta.

"Harry is talking more every day."

"Is that a good thing or a bad thing?"

"Very funny. How's work? James getting any better?," she asked.

"No. And he's still calling me Genny." I let that settle for a minute. To Dad and Annie, I was Lily. To Mom and Aunt Florence, Genevieve. To everyone else, I was Lillian.

I was named after my grandmothers. My parents argued about whose mother's name would be first. With only weeks remaining before the due date, they made a unique compromise. If I was born on an even numbered day, it would be my maternal grandmother's name, then my paternal grandmother's name. If I was born on an odd numbered day, the opposite. I was born on January 4, so Genevieve Lillian it was. However, I was born at 12:01 in the morning. Dad swore my mother adjusted the clock to get her way. He felt wronged and always called me Lillian. Somewhere along the way, it became Lily.

My dad got his revenge when I was five and he brought me to my first day of kindergarten. He introduced me as Lillian to my teacher and classmates. It stuck. I still remember the first day I came home with papers referring to me as Lillian. I had never seen anyone so mad. My mom didn't talk to my dad for two weeks. I think she would have cooled down sooner if he hadn't brought her home flowers a few days afterwards- a bouquet of lilies.

After a long exhale, "I know he sees me cringe every time he says it." My mom would have cringed too at the thought of me as 'Genny.' "I've given up telling him how no one calls me that. Last week, he was quick to point out that patients are now starting to call me that too."

Suppressing a giggle, Annie asked "Are they?"

"Yes," suppressing the desire to scream.

"I still don't understand why James doesn't like you."

"He wants my work shifts."

"How is that your fault? You were told to work the day shift."

"I know. He just feels like when that other PT was fired, he should have taken days and the new hire, me, should take nights. The boss likes it how it is and doesn't want anyone switching."

Everything happened so fast when I was hired. I was hired on the spot, and the boss told "Gen" to show up at seven in the morning, the next day. I was in such a fog back then that I didn't notice James' aggravation. Six months later, he's still unhappy and I'm Genny.

LILY

Wednesday   6:00 a.m.   January 28, 2009

"**...B**ack and better than ever."

There was Mike Greenberg's voice telling me it was time to get up. I could hear the waves gently crashing. I turned towards the window but couldn't see the waves. It was still dark out; the sun wouldn't rise for another hour. It was too dark and too early to do anything.

I turned over and I could see Laude didn't agree. She was bright eyed, ears up, tail wagging, ready to go, literally.

"I think it may be time to cut our losses, pup. It may be time to leave." She tilted her head to the left, as if considering a response. I continued, "The books on grief said not to make any big decisions for four to six months. They said grief clouds the ability to make sound decisions. It's been longer than that. We don't really like it here, do we?" Laude tilted her head to the right. She didn't have any objections with her life. I, on the other hand, didn't like my job, had no local friends, and felt like a outsider in our home. "Ok, we'll think about it. Maybe I'll call one of those recruiters next week."

I rolled out of bed and Laude and I faced another day.

It would be weeks before I learned how this brief conversation with Laude would change my life.

LILY

Thursday   5:00 p.m.   January 29, 2009

My cell phone rang as I walked into my apartment.
"Hi, Annie. I'm just getting in."

"Got stuck at work?"

"Yep, last patient showed up late."

"That was nice of you to see them."

"Wasn't presented as a choice by the office manager." I had learned the hard way not to argue with Rosa. She had the boss on speed dial and had no qualms about using it.

I patted Laude on top of her head and scooped food into her bowl. A red light to my left caught my eye. "Huh, what's this Laude?," forgetting I was on the phone with Annie.

"What? Did she have an accident?"

"No, my perfect puppy does not have accidents. There's something new on my wall." I stepped over to the wall with the new gadget. It was on the hallway wall beyond the kitchen. It was a white, rectangular with a red electronic "0" on the top. Above that, it read "carbon monoxide alarm".

"What are you talking about?," Annie asked.

"Tony must have put it up. It's a carbon monoxide alarm."

"Jeffrey put one of those up in our home when we moved in. Did you ask Tony to do it?"

"No, but I have him on retainer." We laughed. I got tired of leaving him envelopes with money in it every time he helped me out with something in the apartment. I gave him money every month instead. "He put in new smoke detectors a couple weeks ago too. I guess the new ones are better. He had just changed the batteries when the clocks changed in November but I defer to his judgment."

"You don't even change the batteries?," she asked.

"Please, I'm 5' 2". Do you really think I could reach them? Even on the step stool I can't. Do you change them in your house?"

"No, I have a husband for that. And, you're 5' 1"."

"Ouch. You won't give me an inch will you?" Again, we laughed. Some days, it was like we were still in college. She always teased me for being short. I liked to say petite.

"Nope. Speaking of husbands..."

Before she could continue, "Nope, gotta go. Got to read the manual so I know what the numbers mean. Responsible homeowner and all." We had had a nice conversation and I didn't want it ruined by a discussion of my dating life, or lack thereof, the reasons I don't have a boyfriend, or worse, the matchmaking site.

LILY

Friday   4:00 p.m   January 30, 2009

'Thank God It's Friday' had taken a new meaning at my job. So did "dress down Friday". I called it 'dress inappropriately for your age' day. I missed the days of scrubs and sneakers in the hospital I had interned at.
The day had been fairly unmemorable- a steady stream of patients, three to four an hour with various complaints. That was until 90 year old Mr. Bernie Franks asked "What do you think about me driving?" as he stumbled over his cane.

'Terror' was my first thought but I knew it was not the one I should say. "Well, sir, I think that is a discussion with your family and doctor." And while we're talking about it if you could warn me before you start driving I'd appreciate it, was left unsaid.

"Thanks, Genny." I didn't cringe when he called me Genny. He was a sweet man, who was always pleasant and eager to work. He paused as he looked over in the direction of James', his former therapist. "I'm so glad I'm working with you. I really think I'm getting stronger. Plus, you make me laugh." I smiled when he winked at me. I helped him put on his jacket and escorted him to the front waiting room to his daughter, who would safely drive him home.

"You have a good weekend, honey," he said as his daughter held the door open for him. I smiled and waved goodbye.

I handed in my paperwork for the day, clocked out and headed for the door before anyone could stop me. As a whole, the week had been better than most and I wanted it to stay that way. James had been tolerable, mainly focused on the Super Bowl and his party. A party I had conveniently not been invited to. I had a morbid curiosity of what his home looked like. The ladies would fill me in on Monday.

LILY

Saturday   1:00 p.m.   January 31, 2009

Laude and I sat on the patio watching the waves—the ocean was just one block south. I had always found the ocean soothing- the sound of it, the sight of it, the smell of it. As a child, when Mom would drop me off, I'd take a deep breath and Aunt Florence and I would look at it each other and say "Gotta love that smell, baby!" Then we'd giggle and she'd give me a big hug. On nice days, we'd go on the boardwalk that ran parallel to the ocean for two and half miles.

Today, the boardwalk was crowded with walkers, joggers, and bikers. It was unseasonably warm, fifty degrees, sunny. It made me, and probably everyone else forget the snow storm we had earlier in the month.

I returned to reading my book, a supernatural thriller that would probably keep me up most of the night, when my cell phone rang.

"I'm on the patio, enjoying the beautiful weather. You?," I answered.

"The same. Harry and I went to the park. He ran himself out so he'll be napping for a bit. Why aren't you walking on the boardwalk?"

"Laude's not allowed to. I feel bad leaving her. I'm perfectly content reading my book." Hearing her name, she shifted her attention from the busy street to my face. When she didn't hear another word that she liked (treat, potty, good girl), she went back to watching the traffic on Broadway.

"This is why you don't have a boyfriend. You got to get out there, Lily."

"I'm out here." True, but not what she meant.

"I still think you should get a bike. It would be a great way to meet a guy. Plus, good exercise."

"I get enough exercise at work and walking Laude. I think we both remember my incident with a bike in college." We laughed at the memory of me getting run down on the boardwalk by a bicyclist. It was the first day of her weeklong visit after our freshman year. Fortunately, nothing but my pride was hurt.

"You should have looked both ways before crossing the bike path." That made us laugh even harder. It was the same thing my aunt had said to me. Aunt Florence and Annie bonded immediately laughing over my prone body, with a bike track running over my right lower leg.

The bike path ran along the middle of the boardwalk and many bicyclists were ruthless. I often felt like frogger while attempting to traverse it. It was amazing to watch Ms. June cross it, though. She just crossed it and no one ever came close to her.

"Gotta go, Annie. I want to finish this book." I had started it last night and had forced myself to put it down at one in the morning.

"I don't know how you read that stuff."

"This coming from the person who watches every crime drama there is."

"Not every one. And the information may some day come in handy."

"I think the same about these books." We both laughed, knowing that was unlikely. Little did I know.

"Love you, Lily."

"Love ya, Annie."

I resumed reading the book and finished it that night. If I ever woke up in an alternate universe, I would be prepared. I laughed at the thought. I had no idea that two weeks later I would. Nothing could have prepared me for that.

LILY

Sunday   8:30 a.m.   February 1, 2009

"Good morning, Annie." There was only one person I knew that I could call anytime and that was Annie. The joys of motherhood meant Annie was up early on Sunday mornings and I had someone to talk to while I ate breakfast. It was less lonely that way.

She replied, as always on Sunday mornings, "What did you get from the bakery today?" My Sunday morning routine was picking up breakfast at Rein's Bakery a few blocks away. It was Aunt Florence's routine whether I was staying with her or not. It's a hard habit to break.

"Cheese danish. The counter lady told me she really liked my pajama bottoms-the ones you gave me for Christmas."

"Cheese danish sounds good. Better than this cold cereal." I could hear the spoon hit the bowl as she put it back down and imagined her disappointed face that there wasn't a pastry in it.

"Wait...what did you say about pajamas? Please tell me you did not walk three blocks to the bakery in pants with penguins on them?"

Silence. She wouldn't be happy with the truth.

"You know this is why you don't have a boyfriend! You leave the house in your pajamas!"

"I thought it was because I didn't fix my hair before I walked Laude?" Seconds later, I realized silence would have been a better response.

"Your hair wasn't brushed either, was it?," she asked.

Again, she wouldn't be happy with the truth. The silence lasted longer than I expected so I went with the old standby. "I think Laude has to go."

With her voice a little higher than usual, "Lillian, don't you dare hang up that phone. I know she just got back from the walk from the bakery!"

"Gotta go, Annie. Love ya." I thought it was best to hang up then. No point ruining a perfectly good Sunday with an argument. Plus, the danish was waiting.

LILY

Monday   5:00 p.m.   February 2, 2009

"How was your day?" Annie sounded a bit more tired than usual.
"I wore different shoes to work."
"What do you mean? Do you usually wear the same pair everyday?," she asked naively.
I thought it was bad enough I had done it. But having to explain it made it worse.
"I mean I wore two different shoes to work today."
"Please tell me you're kidding."
"No, plus I didn't notice for three hours."
"I know you're kidding." She sounded weary. I expected her to laugh. All I got was silence. Not even my name. I thought it was funny. I got dressed in the dark. These things happen. It's still so dark and so early in the morning when I leave for work. In my defense, they were the same style of shoe but different colors, one light brown and one black.

Trying to get a laugh, I reminded her of the good old days. "You know when we were in college, you would have thought this was funny."
"Yes, when a college kid wears two different shoes it's funny, quirky. When an adult does it, people question their sanity."

"No one noticed." I was relieved that no one had pointed out my error. My co-workers were mostly distracted about re-telling tales of the Super Bowl party and by their hangovers.

"No, no one told you they noticed. There is a difference. This is why you don't have a boyfriend." She sounded exasperated, and not in the usual way that entertained me.

"I thought it was because I wore pajamas to the bakery," I quipped.

Again, I didn't hear the expected laugh. With Harry crying in the background, I was saved from a further lecture. She said goodbye, talk to you later, the usual.

Maybe I should keep a list of all the reasons Annie said I didn't have a boyfriend. Although, I wasn't sure if it would be funny or depressing. I knew it wouldn't be instructive. I could guarantee there would be a lot of reasons. Again, not sure if that was funny or depressing.

LILY

Tuesday   5:00 p.m.   February 3, 2009

Annie's standard opening line. "How was your day?"
"As good as could be expected."
"And what does that mean?"
"That means I listen to people complain all day."
"That's a bit dramatic isn't it? You are there to help them. They have to tell you what hurts."
"Yes, I know. But how can I explain, nicely, to the 50 year old obese woman recovering from arthroscopic knee surgery that her knees hurt because she's fat. She actually asked me why she has not healed in two weeks like the football players."
"I'm not sure if I want to know how you answered that."
"I answered it as nicely as a I could."
There was a pause while she contemplated whether or not to ask. "And that means...."
"First I asked her exactly what type of surgery she thought she had. Because I am unfamiliar with a procedure that would turn a middle aged woman a hundred pounds overweight into a professional athlete."
"Uh-uh."
"She didn't answer so I told her that I doubt she was in football playing shape to begin with. And most importantly, I didn't laugh or even smirk."

"I guess that's good." Annie sounded relieved that I had handled the situation better than she expected.

"Do you really not like it?," she asked seriously.

We both knew I didn't. I liked being a physical therapist but didn't like the office I worked in. Worse, this wasn't "the plan".

Annie's after college plan was to marry Jeffrey and work in advertising, which she did until Harry was born. My plan was to be a travel physical therapist for a year or so to see the country. I'd work three months, or longer if I liked it, at different locations, wherever I wanted to go. It was a way to live in other parts of the country without committing to them long term. I think we both assumed I'd end up in New York, near my parents or in Pennsylvania, near her. I had met a therapist at one of my internships who sold me on the idea. But all that changed the day before I graduated. So, here I was living in an apartment I never expected, in a job I would never like, alone.

I could deflect her with humor, telling her how James had tried to sabotage me at work, again. I could answer her honestly.

"No, it's fine. I'm just tired."

Or I could just lie.

Annie called back to check on me after Harry went to sleep. Instead of making me feel better, she made me feel worse.

She innocently asked, "Have you talked to Aunt Florence?"

The questions about Aunt Florence had slowly decreased over the past few months. I didn't think Annie had asked since Christmas. She always hoped I would say yes and everything would go back to the way it was. We both knew it would not ever be like it was but neither of us understood why Aunt Florence was no longer a part of my life. We knew the when, but not the why.

Annie loved and missed her, too. She had come to visit for a week in the summers in college. We loved sunbathing during the day on the beach. Actually, Annie loved the sunbathing and I loved reading, lathered with SPF 50, under an umbrella. Aunt Florence would take us out to dinner or she would cook. At least one night, she would make Annie's favorite, lobster, while making me something non-seafood. Annie was envious of the close relationship I had with my mother's sister. I looked to Aunt Florence as a second mom; a mom without the lectures, groundings and guilt.

Unfortunately, the answer was the same.

"No, last time I called they said she was out." The good news was that I could now say it without crying. I guess I had run out of tears.

Annie tried not to push but the situation was perplexing. "Why don't you just stop by?"

"I tried on New Years Day but I'm not on the list."

"What do you mean you are not on the list? What list? You're her only niece. Of course, you're on the the list." I wasn't sure if she was more agitated or confounded.

I was sure I was on some list. My dad would have called it "The Shit List." All I knew was I was not on the list at the guard shack to be let into the housing complex where Aunt Florence now lived.

"The guard at the gate said I wasn't on the list and they wouldn't let me in. I thought it was some mistake. I was on it in November. I asked the guard to call her but he said no and made me leave. So, I called and I know I heard her in the background but they said she was out. They wouldn't even let me leave a message."

I had only been to Aunt Florence's new home, in the 55 and older community once, at Thanksgiving. Aunt Florence was horrified and shocked when I arrived. Chloe was equally surprised by her mother's reaction. Chloe had called me the week before to invite me and must have put me on the list with the guard. I overheard them quarelling about my presence, in the bedroom. Charlie seemed to be oblivious to the drama as he watched football and drank his six pack.

"I just don't understand." That made two of us.

LILY

Wednesday   7:00 p.m.   February 4, 2009

I was lounging on the couch, Laude stretched across my legs when the phone rang. I could hear Harry babbling in the background when I answered it. "Hi, Harry."

"Say hi to Aunt Lily." I heard a mix of sounds that sounded nothing like hi or aunt or Lily. I had a bad feeling that one day over the next year he would call me something that Annie would find endearing and I would find horrible. Aunt Lala or something worse. Although I could guarantee it wouldn't be Aunt Genny. Just the thought of that sent a shiver down my spine.

"Ok, go with Daddy, he'll put you to bed." I heard Annie kiss him before asking "What are you doing?"

"I'm on the computer."

"Oh, good you're getting started on the matchmaking site."

Silence.

There she was again, the overbearing mother. I still didn't know why this persona appeared, if it was because she became a mother or because I lost mine and she thought I needed a substitute when my life went into free fall.

Part of me was surprised she still asked about the dating website. After four weeks, I thought it was quite clear I was never going to do it.

"Can I take the silence as 'No, Annie. Although I greatly appreciate this thoughtful gift that could be life changing, I am not on the dating site filling out the survey, filling out my profile'?"

A simple yes would suffice. It had been a long day and I wasn't up for a lecture or a disagreement.

"Yes, that would be correct Annie."

"Why not? And don't try to be funny."

"I don't *try* to be funny. I just am."

"I'm waiting." Annie said it in that motherly tone, the no nonsense tone. God help Harry when he got older. I could hear it now "Harold Brian get down here." At least, for me, there was no name calling yet. Operative word, yet.

She didn't want funny so she got the truth. "I read that someone should not make big, life changing decisions after a traumatic event. I believe you gave me the book."

"First of all, Lillian, going out on a date is not a 'big, life changing decision'."

"For me, it is."

Ignoring me, she continued, "Second of all, it said someone should not make any major decisions for four to six months after a big loss."

"Well, I had two big losses simultaneously. So that gives me a year." I thought my logic was sound.

"Lil, just because they died doesn't mean you did too."

There it was. Neither of us usually said it out loud. We usually danced around it, my parents deadly car crash. Instead of moving to Virginia and starting my career as a travel physical therapist seeing the country, I moved back to New York after graduation.

Aunt Florence sold my parents' home, my childhood home, and gave me her apartment while she moved into a fifty five and older community. She arranged the job interview at the outpatient facility.

Sometimes, it seemed like I went to sleep May 25 with sweet dreams of graduation and the future and woke up July 1, alone.

"If they could talk to you now, what do you think they would say?" I was not sure which I liked less. Annie being serious or telling me why I didn't have a boyfriend.

"They'd say they were glad I have Laude." It wasn't the answer she was looking for but we both knew it was the truth.

"How she survived the accident we'll never know," Annie said. At least that got her off dating, although probably only temporarily.

"Can you imagine the police officer's face when he found her sitting by the side of the road? A little pup with the pink bow and collar? Not even a scratch on her. What a cute name too? She'd still be nameless if they hadn't put the tag on her collar."

Aunt Florence told me the card had said "To Our Cum Laude graduate, a little 'Laude' to remind you daily of us while you are seeing the world. Love, Mom and Dad." The card was never found. Thankfully, Laude was. It was the last, and best, gift they ever gave me. It was the only good thing that had happened to me over the past eight months. I'd like to forget May 26 but I'd never forget Aunt Florence being pulled into my hotel room by the two pound schnauzer puppy.

I remembered my range of emotions at that moment as if it was yesterday. First, I was puzzled, not knowing who the dog was. Then, elation when I realized she was mine. My elation and smile didn't last when I saw Aunt Florence's face and I saw that she was alone.

I was pulled back to the present by Jeffrey's voice in the background, something about Harry's blanket.

"Oh, Jeffrey needs me. Talk to you later Lily. I love you."

"Love you, too," I replied but she had already hung up.

And there I was, alone, again. Except for Laude, who remained stretched across my legs. I knew it was not Annie's intention to bring me back to painful places, but I would spend the rest of the night thinking about graduation and the following six weeks. Aunt Florence and Annie made me go to graduation. "That's what they would have wanted," they said.

The police had informed Aunt Florence initially. They had found her name and information in the wreckage. The night before graduation, she had been staying in the hotel with her son, Charlie, two floors below Annie and me. Aunt Florence's daughter, Chloe, and her family were on another floor. Everyone had come to see me graduate. My parents had reservations at the hotel but never checked in. They had gotten delayed getting Laude from the breeder.

I had spent the night celebrating with Annie, going to our old favorite places. We got in around midnight. Our outfits for the next day were pressed and hanging in the closet. Everyone was going to have breakfast together before the ceremony. I was in my pajamas, starting to doze, when I heard the knock on the door. I thought it was Mom, coming to tell me she and Dad had arrived. Annie let Aunt Florence and Laude in. That's the last coherent image I have of that night.

Aunt Florence handled everything. The funeral, the insurance, the sale of the house and whatever else goes with death. After settling everything, she said there was no money left and I could take her home. I thought she meant I could live with her until I got my bearings. When I got to her apartment, she handed me the keys and the deed and started to leave. She said I needed to get a job to pay the monthly maintenance fee, as well as utilities. She was moving to an adult community. I had to stop her in the hallway to ask for her new phone number and address. I thought at the time she was going to leave without giving either. Now, I knew she would have.

Looking back, I could see how Aunt Florence was different after their death. At the time, I was too consumed by my own grief to notice anything. I was so glad she was there to take care of all the minutia. But, she was not there to help me emotionally. Annie did that.

I may never know why she did not want me in her life anymore. I was her only niece; her little sister's only child. When I was born, her children were teenagers. She always told me I was like another one of her children but better, because I could be returned. She laughed at that.

My parents only lived thirty minutes away and I spent many weekends and most of the summers with her. How could we go from that to this? Maybe, she looked at me and saw her only sister, and wanted to forget. Maybe she blamed me. If I hadn't been graduating they would have never been on that rural road that night. Annie said everyone processed grief differently and she would come around. I wasn't so sure. I was starting to believe Aunt Florence was gone, like the rest of my family.

LILY

Thursday   5:00 p.m.   February 5, 2009

I walked into my apartment after another long workday. The highlight of coming home was Laude. She was always so happy to see me. Running back and forth, tail wagging, jumping up. But today was different. After a few laps, while I went to get her a treat, she sat. I gave her a treat and she raised her paw.

The phone rang. "Hi, Annie," I answered.

"What are you doing?," she asked with Harry giggling in the background.

"Shaking Laude's hand."

"I'm impressed. When did you teach her that?" Annie had been less than impressed with my dog training skills during a previous visit. I did point out that Laude was house trained and she agreed that was most important.

"I didn't." I just sat on the floor with Laude and shook her hand, astonished. I gave her another treat and she was off to her bed to eat it.

"If you didn't teach her, how did you learn she could do it?" Good question.

"I guess Susie taught her. I would be happy if I could get her to sit consistently, never thought to teach her any tricks. I came home today and during her greeting process, she sat down and raised her paw. So I shook it."

"Curious, but that's cute."

I put my coat away and went into the kitchen and stared into the cupboard trying to decide on dinner. I could hear Annie rattling around her kitchen too. Needing inspiration, I asked, "What's for dinner?"

"Pureed chicken and squash."

Not an inspiring answer. "I meant for you and Jeffrey. I'm really not in the mood for mush." I had a flashback of my patient's meals from my internship at a rehabilitation center. For some, it was completely pureed and completely unappetizing. Maybe I wasn't hungry after all.

I heard Annie laugh and tell Harry "Aunt Lily doesn't like the sounds of your dinner. What do you have to say to that?" On cue, he made a raspberry. The perfect response.

"Leftovers for us. Chinese from last night." That sounded good but would require me going back out and it was cold and starting to snow. "You?"

I opened the freezer to check out other options. "Frozen pizza." It was the only thing that looked appetizing in the freezer.

"This is why you don't have a boyfriend. You have to learn to cook. You know what they say, the way to a man's heart is through his stomach."

"I don't remember that being how you landed Jeffrey. I remember plenty of nights of takeout. I also remember how you first met him."

That made us both giggle. She met him as a side effect of a dare. A party prank gone wrong if I had done it. For Annie, it led to her meeting her future husband.

"Don't say it. Harry will always think we met at a college social."

"What, nothing about flashing?" It was mardi gras and it sounded like a good idea.

"I said don't say it!" And we both laughed as we flash-backed to her flashing the young Jeffrey walking past our dorm window. We never thought he'd see, never mind laugh and come closer to the window to say hello.

As the giggling settled down, Annie changed topics. In hindsight, I should have ended the conversation on our good laugh.

"You know I was thinking, maybe you should call Charlie or Chloe to see what's going on with Aunt Florence. Maybe there's something wrong."

There was plenty wrong with the whole situation and we both knew it. Talking to my cousins wasn't going to make anything right. Fifteen to eighteen years between us, we never had anything in common and didn't spend a lot of time together- holidays and birthdays only. When I started staying at Aunt Florence's, they were already adults, living on their own. Chloe lived in Connecticut with her family- husband (now ex-) and two children. Charlie was doing whatever he does. The only image I had of Charlie was him drinking beer and asking Aunt Florence for money, which she always gave him.

"I talked to Chloe before Christmas and she was pretty short with me on the phone. One word answers for everything. I think she's a little overwhelmed with the single mother role." It had been an awkward conversation. I had called to find out what the holiday plans were. Every year, all of us would go to midnight mass at St. Mary of the Isle in Long Beach, after a late dinner at Aunt Florence's. We would have Christmas Day dinner at my parent's home. I told myself her detached attitude was because of the divorce but I knew better.

"And Charlie?"

He had acted oddly at the funeral. He didn't seem too upset about their death. He was more upset about needing a car. Aunt Florence handled that too.

"We never spoke at the funeral and we haven't spoken since." That wasn't exactly true. He had called me once after I had moved into the condo. He was yelling and screaming, obviously drunk, that it should be his place, not "some little spoiled brat's." He continued with "You've got a job, get your own fucking place." I hung up after that. No need for Annie to know about that.

"Wait, did you say you talked to Chloe 'before Christmas'? Wasn't she at Aunt Florence's on Christmas?"

She had missed my slip yesterday about November being the last time I was on the guest list at Aunt Florence's place. It was a record that I had gotten away with a lie with Annie for six weeks. I didn't want Annie to know I had spent Christmas alone. She had invited me to her home but I had to work Christmas Eve and December 26. That gave James a Merry Christmas right there. He did everything he could to get as many patients as possible to schedule appointments during those shifts. It would have been too tough to drive back and forth to her place in between. Plus, I didn't want to intrude on Harry's first Christmas. She didn't push the issue when I said I was going to Aunt Florence's. She was happy at the prospect of me having Christmas with my family and hopeful it would get things back to normal.

She took "fine" as an appropriate answer when she asked about Christmas. No follow-up questions. We were both more than pleased to talk about Harry's Christmas and how much he loved all his gifts, especially the ones from "Aunt Lily."

"I don't know. I'm sure she was. But I wasn't." I paused not wanting to admit why I wasn't there. "I wasn't invited."

I heard her take a few breaths as she struggled to find something to say. "I'm sorry."

"Me too."

LILY

Friday   8:00 p.m.   February 6, 2009

Laude was sitting by the patio door watching the snow start to fall. Second only to watching the ocean, I loved watching snow fall; especially, when I had nowhere to go. I should be embarrassed as a twenty three year old single woman that on a Friday night I was in my pajamas. But, I wasn't. Annie would be embarrassed enough for me.

I had called some recruiters today and they were going to call me back with some options.

Laude was very excited when I told her when I got home. It may have been the treat I was holding while I told her all about it. We shook on it.

Snow was forecasted to fall most of the night, leaving us with close to a foot. I thought it best to take Laude out now before the snow was higher than her. I sang her favorite song. "It's potty time. Ya, it's potty time. Oh, what a night." She probably only liked the word "potty" repeated several times or the fact that a walk always followed my awful singing. Regardless, she was excited at the prospect of a walk. I was excited at the prospect of a new start.

In two weeks, I could be living a new life. It turned out to be a week, and not of my own doing.

LILY

Sunday   7:30 a.m.   February 8, 2009

My cell phone rang as I was putting the key in the building's front door. I answered, "Too early this morning, Annie. I'm not home from the bakery yet. I'm just walking back into the building. And the elevator is waiting."

"Please tell me the open elevator doesn't still freak you out." Annie used to think my quirkiness was humorous; now, not so much.

"It does. I don't think that's odd. An elevator door should open when you press the button."

"Its called a sensor. You read too many supernatural novels."

"Not possible." Laude and I stepped on the elevator and pressed five.

"Before you tell me about your bakery choice, let me..."

"Russian tea biscuit." I interrupted her before she could ask me about what I looked like. I knew she would not like the answer. 'Russian tea biscuit' would distract her.

"Ooh, my favorite." I knew this. We even experimented making them, but that didn't go well. Something always went wrong between rolling out the dough, filling it with raspberry jam, walnuts, and golden raisins, and topping it with cinnamon sugar.

"I know and it's delicious. How's that cold cereal?" My breakfast was the only aspect of my day that would top hers.

"Ugh. What did you do last night?"

I stepped off the elevator and headed to our apartment where coffee was waiting.

"Watched a movie. Contemplated the meaning of life."

She laughed, "What movie did you watch?"

"Weekend at Bernie's." A movie we had watched one too many times in college. From the moment we pressed play, we laughed. The best lines we said in unison with Larry and Richard, through our laughter.

"Why don't you come down next weekend and we'll watch something better."

"And by that, you mean any other movie."

"Exactly." And neither of us could stop laughing, again. I could hear Harry join the giggle-fest.

"Can we do the following weekend? They're predicting another big storm and Laude has a check-up."

"Oh, that's what I meant. We have Jeffrey's brother's wedding this weekend."

I had forgotten that was this weekend. I initially had asked if she wanted me to go along to watch Harry since Annie and Jeffrey were both in the bridal party. I was relieved when she had declined.

"We won't be able to talk for a few days. You know my cell doesn't work up there."

"You'll be fine," I assured her. "You'll just have to talk to your husband."

"Very funny. You know that's not what I meant."

"I have the hotel's number and your mother in law's number. Really, Annie, it's just a few days." I tried to assuage her concerns but I had to admit, it would be weird. I couldn't remember going more than a day without talking to Annie since we met freshman year. She even called me every day on her honeymoon. "Just enjoy the wedding!"

"Pretty cheesy, huh? Valentine's Day wedding." We laughed, just as we did when she got the save the date card. Looking back, a Valentine's Day wedding would have been an ideal destination compared to where I was that day.

LILY

Monday   February 9, 2009

Knowing my time at my job was limited made Monday fly by. I knew within the month I would be gone. Olivia assured me there were a few positions available, with start dates as soon as I could get there. Once I accepted a job, I'd give my two weeks notice and be gone.

I hadn't told Annie yet and felt guilty about that. But I hadn't fully made up my mind and nothing was signed, yet. She had helped me the first time around. While newborn Harry napped in his nursery, we looked at a map and routed a plan of assignments across the country over a year. I would start in Virginia, then spend the winter in Arizona, the spring in Chicago, and the summer in Oregon. On paper, it sounded great. We both knew it wouldn't work out exactly as planned but looked forward to adjusting it as the year progressed.

I didn't need Annie's help formulating a new plan. I was doing the old plan, it was just delayed nine months.

Laude was fully behind the plan, and that was all that mattered.

LILY

Tuesday   5:00 p.m.   February 10, 2009

Our pre-dinner chat started differently than usual and that should have been my cue to hang up. Before I could even say hello, Annie said, "You want the good news or the better news?" She sounded ridiculously happy. The only time I had heard her happier was when she booked the band she wanted for her wedding.

"The better news."

I expected her to tell me Harry did something funny and that she got it on video. I should have asked who the good and better news was for. It couldn't be for me.

"You have a date Saturday."

"What? You live two hours away, how could you arrange a date for me? You know Laude has a vet appointment Saturday morning. I told you I can't visit."

Annie began humming that awful tune. A tune that kept me up nights. And then the jingle. "Journey to Love...." I couldn't listen. It could not be true.

"How? I never logged on. I don't even know how to log on. I don't have a username, a password." I was beginning to ramble, to panic.

Annie didn't need to answer because I knew she had done it. The idea had entered my mind but I never really thought she would do it. She had not asked about it in a week. I thought she had given up. I should have known that was too good to be true.

"You'll meet him Saturday at seven at Lucy's on Riverside for dinner."

"No way, no Saturday, no dinner."

"Yes, it's all set."

"No, it is not. That is too much pressure." Then the pressure went up even higher, when I realized, *"Saturday is Valentine's Day!"* I tried not to scream but was unsuccessful.

"Yes, I know. It's perfect." I pictured her standing in her living room. Lovingly looking at her wedding photos on the wall, a diehard romantic.

"No, no, no. I am not going out to dinner with a stranger on Valentine's Day."

"Yes, you are."

"No, I am not." We could do this all night. My only hope was Harry would start to cry and she would give in. The silence lasted and Harry did not come to my rescue.

Begrudgingly, I said "I will compromise with you." I hesitated, not wanting to compromise at all. Watching Laude with her bone, I was reminded of Annie and this website. "I will meet this man for coffee next week."

Silence. At least she was thinking about it.

"Ok, I'll talk to him and reschedule," she sighed.

I heard a distant male voice say "I told you she wouldn't like it." I wasn't sure if Jeffrey meant the whole dating website as a birthday gift or the date specifically. It didn't matter. I didn't like either.

"Wait, what's the good news?"

"You don't have to fill out the matching questionnaires. I did it for you."

We had very different definitions of good news.

LILY

Wednesday　　　*6:00 p.m.*　　　*February 11, 2009*

I had avoided Annie's earlier phone calls but knew I couldn't do it all day. After pleasantries were exchanged, with as much pleasantness I could muster, Annie told me "Ok, you are all set."

I found that hard to believe. "Explain." I was still angry about the whole situation but hoped if I went on one date she would let the matter drop and not fix me up again. I had no idea how right I was.

"You will meet him Friday at seven at Roasters."

"Doesn't it worry you that he could change the date so easily. I mean he doesn't have any plans on Friday night just a few days before the weekend."

"And what are your plans for the weekend, other than walking Laude?"

"At least I would have had enough self respect to lie."

"He's excited to meet you. That's a good sign." I didn't think Annie could sound any happier.

"What does he sound like? Look like?"

"Check out the website for his photo. You should check out his profile anyway. You want to have a few conversation starters going in. You know, sound interested in him."

Considering I didn't know my username and password, it was unlikely I would be getting on the website to see his profile and picture. Since I wasn't interested, nothing could make me sound like it.

I naively thought I could tolerate one disaster date to get Annie off the topic of dating.

"And I don't know what he sounds like," she admitted. "Posing as you on the website is bad enough. I can't sound like you on the phone."

"So, you have set me up with a complete stranger. He could be lying about his profile. The picture could be anyone."

"It is not an inexpensive site so I can't imagine that anyone would waste their time by putting up a fake photo or not being accurate with their profile." She was more delusional than I thought. "You were very accurate in yours. And he really liked your picture."

Oh my God! I hadn't thought about what photo she had used. I debated whether to ask. I decided I'd let her decide. "Do I want to know what picture you used?"

"One of the ones from your December visit."

That could mean a lot of different pictures. After Harry's birth, Annie had purchased a state of the art camera and she used it often. There were pictures of me with Harry and Santa, pictures of me feeding Harry, pictures of me covered in pureed peas, pictures of me and Annie. But I didn't ask for clarification. Her plot had become crystal clear. Her idea to go for "makeovers" was more of a ruse than I had originally thought. I thought she was trying to cheer me up with the holidays approaching. Jeffrey watched Harry and we went shopping for new outfits. We got our makeup done at the stylish new cosmetic store. I thought it was too much makeup but everyone assured me I looked great. I didn't believe the consultant was a reliable source. She wanted me to buy everything for a big commission and went on and on about the colors, creams and brushes. Her co-workers agreed to help her cause, as she slathered on the mascara. But I believed Annie when she said I looked nice; that I just wasn't used to wearing makeup.

In our new outfits, we went out to dinner with Jeffrey and Harry. Looking back, I think she hoped I'd meet my "Mr. Right" in the restaurant and we'd all live happily ever after in Philadelphia. Before dinner arrived she asked Jeffrey how I looked, and he said "Good, if she wants to work on a street corner."

I laughed, gave Annie my best "I told you so" look and went to the ladies room to wash my face. Unfortunately for me, pictures were taken prior to going out.

I could hear Jeffrey laughing in the background. He knew I knew what pictures were used. The rat. "Tell Jeffrey I expected more from him."

LILY

Friday   *6:30 p.m.*   *February 13, 2009*

I could hear the giddiness in Annie's voice when she asked, "Ok, are you ready?"

"For what?"

"The date."

"It's coffee. What's to be ready for?"

"You got my email regarding what to wear right?"

I thought I might as well have a little fun before the date. "Yes, I got the text message and voice mail, too. There was no mention of underwear which I found odd."

"Lillian, don't start."

"Initially, I thought that meant I should use my own judgement but then I remembered you question that frequently so maybe you meant to leave it off."

"*Genevieve Lillian*, I am trying to help you." And that made it all worth it. For some reason hearing Genevieve Lillian spoken through clenched teeth was calming.

"I am trying to get all of us packed for the wedding and it's snowing and Jeffrey's running late."

Again, I had forgotten. Jeffrey's brother's wedding was somewhere in north central Pennsylvania. I did not envy her five hour ride to Coudersport, made longer with the snow. Or an extended weekend in a snow covered town in the middle of the mountains, with no cell phone service.

"Just call me when you get home. We'll still be in the car and I should still have cell phone service. I want to hear all about it."

I highly doubted she would like to hear all about it. This was not going to be good. I could just feel it. Friday the 13th. The horror movie was about to begin.

8 p.m.

As I was walking into the building, I made the obligatory call. I figured I might as well get it over with. Annie picked up on the first ring. "So, tell me! I can't wait to hear all about it!" She paused and added "You are home a little early, though."

"It doesn't take long to drink a cup of coffee."

"Well, its good to leave him wanting more. Tell me everything!" Sadly, she expected a good report.

"He had crazy eyes."

"What?"

"You heard me- *crazy* eyes."

"He had nice blue eyes. It was so striking against his black hair."

"I'm not sure what you're talking. Black hair? All I know is his blue eyes looked crazy."

"Ok, crazy eyes aside, how did it go?"

Astonished, I yelled "'*Aside from crazy eyes.*' You can't get past something like that!" I had been wrong. I thought that if I went on the date Annie would give up for a while. She would see I wasn't ready. I should have known she wouldn't give up that easily.

"What? You're kidding. I hope you didn't let that keep you from getting to know him."

"Annie, I'm awful tired. We'll talk about it tomorrow." I yawned, not knowing how I could be so tired. I had feared the cup of coffee Franklin had bought me would keep me up most of the night.

She continued, "He was really nice. We emailed several times and he was funny, nice, and smart. I thought you'd love him."

As I approached the elevators, the one on the right opened, I screamed. "Just stop! I am not some charity case that desperately needs a man to take care of me. You have to lay off! I cannot take this anymore!" and I hung up on her. I didn't even try to feign an excuse. In all our years as friends, I had never hung up on her. I had used Laude as an excuse many times but always said 'I'll talk to you later' or 'I love you' or something nice or funny before clicking off. Not this time. She pushed too far. I needed her to be my friend again. My mother was gone and I did not need or want a replacement.

I'd call back later to apologize once I cooled down but right now I just couldn't deal with it.

I had no idea how much I would regret hanging up on her.

LILY

Saturday   February 14, 2009

I woke with a terrible headache. The pounding reminded me of the night Annie and I discovered the potency and, the next morning, the after effects of martinis. The smile that thought brought to my face quickly faded when the throbbing intensified.

    I feared opening my eyes. Not sure if that would make my head hurt worse and scared what I would see. I tried to recall my evening. I didn't remember going to bed. Truth was, I didn't remember coming home. Correction, I remembered getting on the elevator. And, arguing on the phone with Annie, before getting on the elevator. But that was it. No getting into my apartment; no getting into my bed. I was trying to remember more when I remembered the most important thing, Laude.

    I gradually opened my eyes and there she was. Sitting right next to me, staring at me. Her ears, which usually stood straight up, were down. Her head was down, too. Not exactly cowering but not the usual morning, happy to see you posture of my puppy. It was a bit disconcerting to see those two dark eyes fixed on me, never mind not knowing how long they had been staring at me.

    It was strange she hadn't asked to go out yet. On weekday mornings, the alarm went off so early that neither of us were awake. On weekend mornings, I usually awoke to a paw tapping my arm and little yips if her initial attempts did not get me up.

I rolled over slowly, hoping slow movements would not increase the pain in my head, to see what time it was. The clock glowed '9:30', much later than our usual six in the morning wake up.

Something seemed off but I couldn't tell what it was. I quickly surveyed the room. Nightstand, dresser, pictures, everything looked fine. Except the shade was down; no wonder I had slept so late. The ocean sounded strong today, too. The waves, a block away, crashed on the shore louder than usual. Remembering the weather forecast, it must be from the impending storm.

"Time to go, Laude," I said. But she didn't move. I rolled out of bed and my feet felt the cushion of the carpet. Especially on cold mornings like this, I was glad Aunt Florence had chosen carpet instead of hardwood floors in the bedroom. The carpet felt even cushier this morning.

I looked down at my pajamas. They were my least favorite set, blue flannel, buttoned down the front and long sleeved. I always felt too warm to sleep in them. I didn't feel warm now though. I thought I had put the pajamas in the laundry earlier in the week but they looked clean, and even pressed—I didn't even own an iron. Annie would attest to that.

"It's potty time, Laude." She just sat there on the bed, staring at me.

"You feeling alright? Don't worry, the vet appointment will be just fine. If we leave now we can just make it." She couldn't possibly know she had a veterinarian appointment today. She may have become my constant companion over the past eight months but she was still a dog with a limited vocabulary, despite the amount I spoke to her.

I decided I would get dressed and even brush my hair. "Never know if there'll be a cute vet right, Laude?" I'd been listening to Annie too much. I smiled at the thought. I had to call her. Hopefully she wasn't too mad about me hanging up on her. I was surprised she hadn't called me yet. I looked around the room and couldn't locate my cell phone.

I walked over to the window to raise the shade to let in the sun and to look at the ocean. But, the ocean wasn't there.

I told myself not to panic. I had to be dreaming and would wake up shortly. There was nothing else that could explain my bedroom window covered with a child-like rendering of the ocean. I had raised the shade expecting to see my windows; windows that looked out to the ocean. Instead, I found a piece of plywood, about the size of my windows. I could only assume it was painted to resemble my view.

My heart now joined my head's pounding. If I just pinched myself, I would wake up in my bed. I pinched myself but I remained where I was. I went back to get Laude but laid back down instead. I held her close and willed myself back to sleep. She didn't protest. I tried to convince myself that closing my eyes and going back to sleep would end the nightmare. Moments later, "GOOD MORNING VALENTINES!" blared from the walls. Startled, I fell out of bed. And I knew this was no dream. The nightmare was real.

I got up and back onto the bed. I clung to Laude and looked desperately around the room. The room that looked just like my room, but somehow wasn't. It couldn't be. The walls in the building were thin and I often could hear my neighbors but nothing like this.

"Sorry, that was a little loud. Again, good morning my valentines!" The unfamiliar male voice spoke again, but at a lower volume. The voice wasn't coming from the other side of the bedroom door. It was somehow coming from the walls even though I couldn't see any speakers.

"I'm waiting," he cheerfully added.

I wasn't sure what he was waiting for, but I was waiting for it all to make sense.

"Well, I'm sure Laude has to potty. Come on, Laude."

We both just sat there on what I had thought was my bed. The cherry sleigh bed that looked just like mine, covered with the white and light blue geometrical patterned duvet. I pulled the covers and Laude close.

How did he know her name? The first easy question of the day - her collar. Her identification tag and collar both had her name on it. I had thought a pink crystal collar with her name on it was cute. Annie had thought it was a sign I needed money management classes.

"It's potty time, Laude." He then hummed the tune I sang to her on weekend mornings. I was never cheerful enough for song on weekday mornings. No one knew I sang to her. Annie would have teased me unmercifully if she knew I sang to Laude. Never mind that I had made up up the lyrics set to the tune to The Four Season's song "Oh, what a night." How did he know that?

He stopped humming long enough to say, "Just send her through the door."

I looked to the left at the bedroom door and saw the second thing that was different from my room. There was a small doggie door in the standard door.

My voice waivered, "She's used to me taking her. She's not going to go with you." I looked around the room in anticipation of his reply.

He tried to reassure me. "She'll be just fine."

I didn't know what to do. I certainly wasn't going to let Laude out of my sight, never mind go out with someone who, at best, was delusional.

I got off the bed and put Laude on the floor. She stayed close by my side, unusual for her this early in the morning. She usually ran around while I tried to get her leash on. I went over to the door to get a closer look. I got on my hands and knees and started to push the flap out to see what was on the other side.

"Come on, Laude!" I jumped in surprise. This time the voice didn't come from a speaker but from the other side of the door. This time, Laude obeyed. She ran through the flap. Stunned, I went to grab her but the flap closed and I heard a click. I pushed on it and it wouldn't budge. I was alone.

I desperately looked around the room. The paralyzing shock that began when I had returned to bed ended. I pounded on the door and screamed, "Anyone there? Please let me out!" I yelled until I cried and fell to the floor. I kicked and kicked the unyielding dog door. Exhausted, I leaned against the wall.

For what seemed like forever, but was only fifteen minutes according to the bedside clock, I waited for Laude's return. I stared at the clock, trying to recall the evening. I could only remember hanging up on Annie.

I heard a click and Laude came running in. I stayed on the floor and just watched her.

"See, she was just fine. She likes me." I heard him say from the other side of the door. She did seem fine. She had started her usual after morning walk ritual of running around. I wasn't sure if I wanted to see what was on the other side of the door but I did have to go the bathroom too.

"Excuse me. Um, I have to go, too."

"Oh, sorry. You didn't find it? Of course, you wouldn't look in the closet for the bathroom right. So silly of me." Again through the speakers, I could hear him. I sat there and tried to process how normal he sounded. There wasn't anything distinctive about his voice. He sounded like most of the men I talked to on a typical day, with a mild New York accent.

"Come on, get up and go in the closet. Well, bathroom but what you thought was a closet." I could hear the smile in his voice. He thought this was funny.

I got up slowly and with Laude at my feet, I walked over to the closet/bathroom door. I put my hand on the doorknob but hesitated. This was a man that could truly have skeletons in his closet and I was afraid to find them. Laude barked and I jumped. I looked down and she was just looking at me, head cocked to the side.

"She's telling you to open the door," he said. I had thought the same thing.

After taking care of the necessities, I was greeted by the stranger's voice again. "I have to go out for a while. I have a big night planned for us. Our first *official* date on Valentine's Day no less!" A first date on Valentine's Day was terrifying enough, never mind one with a crazy person.

"Just make yourself at home!," followed by the creepiest laugh I had ever heard.

Minutes later, I heard a car start and drive away. After that the only thing I could hear were waves; occasionally a seagull. It wasn't the peaceful sound of waves crashing on the shore I had become accustomed to over the past seven months. And I never heard seagulls at home. I closed my eyes and listened. I didn't hear any planes. I always heard planes headed to or from John F. Kennedy Airport flying close to Long Beach. I could hear them regularly over my building at home. I didn't know what was beyond the window in this room, but the lack of noise told me I wasn't in Long Beach. No buses; no people's voices; no cars. I tried to locate the source of the ocean sounds. I couldn't see any speakers on the ceiling. Only a smoke detector, like mine, positioned in the same place. I stood on the bed just to be sure.

I got down and crawled around the room. I found the speaker wedged between the wall and my dresser. I mean, the dresser. The dresser that looked remarkably like the one that had been in my old room, the one Aunt Florence had moved into the condo when she moved out. On my hands and knees, I could smell the fresh paint from the wall. The wiring came through the wall. I tugged on the wiring but it wouldn't budge.

I couldn't find a way out. I had spent two hours trying, in between bouts of yelling and crying. I had paced the twenty by ten foot space in hopes of finding an exit. Like my own bedroom, there were only two ways out of the room - the door and the window. The door was dead bolted. The door opened out so I had no access to the hinges. I kicked and pounded on the door with no results. With a running start, I ran into the door. The result was me on the floor, holding my arm, in pain. The door didn't feel a thing.

Still on the floor, I looked closely at the doggie door. It was as solid as the door itself and didn't budge when I pushed on it. It was too small for me to fit through anyway. If Laude got much bigger she wouldn't even fit through it.

I got up to take a closer look at the wood covering the window. Most disturbingly, it was painted like the ocean. At least, the view of the ocean from my apartment, seen through some very strange eyes. It had the boardwalk, with a few dots on it, which I could only assume were to resemble people. I was no art critic but it was bad. Besides the fact that it was a poor reflection of my beautiful ocean view, the whole thing had an odd feel. The perspective was off. I had no doubt there were a few things off about the artist.

The painting was held securely in place by nails. I couldn't find anything in the room to try to get the nails out. I banged on it and wondered if there was a window behind the wood. I pulled out a dresser drawer, dumping out the underwear it held. I took it and threw it against the window. The only result was the drawer fell to the floor, broken.

I looked down at Laude who was at my feet. "Any ideas?" She stared at me for a moment and then got up and ran around with her purple octopus toy in her mouth. I took that to mean "Play along" which became my new plan.

Despite the sheer terror I had awakened to, I was now bored. As I stared at the "window', I re-thought my firm belief that a television did not belong in the bedroom.

I had found food for Laude and myself. The refrigerator was just as oddly placed as everything else. It was in the closet next to the bedroom door. The shoe closet in my bedroom. Instead I found a small refrigerator on the bottom, that other than its size, was like mine. It was stocked with many of the same items I had in mine- peanut butter, jelly, bread, bottled water. On the top shelves of the closet, were other staples, plastic silver wear, paper plates, mugs, soup, cereal, Laude's food, and a microwave. It was all too clear that this wasn't a crime of impulse. And he expected me to be here a while. I wasn't sure if that was a good thing or a bad thing.

At five in the evening, I heard a car pull up. Within five minutes, the voice was back on the speakers. "Happy Valentine's Day!" I had never heard a man so excited about this particular holiday.

I was looking in the direction of the speaker when I heard the click of the doggie door. "Come on Laude. Let's go potty," and she went running through the door. Before I heard the flap slap closed, a box was pushed through. A red gift-wrapped box, with a big red bow. With nothing else to do but wait for Laude's return, I opened it. I found a red jersey knit dress and black heels. Not exactly my style but it was my size.

When Laude returned, he said "I'll pick you up at six."

"Playing along" meant changing into my gift and waiting to be picked up. I could only hope we were going out and I could run. I just had to convince him to let me take Laude.

At precisely, six o'clock there was a knock at the door. I was ready in the outfit I was given. The dress was fitted, but not tight, and came to just above my knees. The heels were high but not uncomfortable. In another place, I would have been happy to go out in this although I doubt I would have chosen it for myself. The bright red color and the form fitting silhouette was complementary but would have attracted more attention than I was normally looking for.

He knocked again. I had no way to open the door so I just waited. Not knowing what else to do, I asked "Who is it?"

The door opened and there he was, dressed in an expensive grey suit, holding two long stemmed roses, one red and one white, in his hands. I had envisioned a lot of things on the other side of the door. What I absolutely expected to see was a stranger, but I didn't.

The good news was Annie would never set me up again. The bad news was I may never get the chance to let her.

"Hi, I'm Craig. It is so nice to finally, officially, meet you. I have heard, I mean read, so many good things about you!" He might have been "Craig" tonight but last night he was Franklin. Different name, same crazy eyes.

"Here's one for you and one for Laude." He handed me the red rose and put the white one in Laude's collar.

Despite my shock, I did my best. "Thank you."

"You look beautiful."

"Thank you," I stuttered. I didn't remember a man ever telling me I looked beautiful. Pretty or nice, but never beautiful.

"Ready to go?" and he pointed up the stairs that lay beyond the bedroom door.

With Laude at my heels, I answered, "Sure, can Laude come?"

He smiled. "Of course, I know you don't go anywhere without her."

That was easier than I expected but I was quickly disappointed when he escorted us to a candle lit table set for two.

The rest of the house looked nothing like my home. The door at the top of the basement stairs opened to a foyer. The front door was to my left. I tried not to stare at it but it beckoned to me- my exit, my way out of this house. Before I could contemplate an escape, "Craig" had a hold of my arm. It was light, for now. But I knew if I made a break for it, he could easily hold me back. I would need a sizable lead to escape.

Last night, all I had noticed about him were his eyes. Blue piercing eyes that watched me too intently. Other than that I had found him relatively average- average build, average hair with above average height. At the coffee house, his brown hair was slicked back. It had made him look more intense. Tonight, it was short in the back and sides, the top was cut jaggedly, pointed in all directions. The popular, effortless style that took longer to fix than my own hair.

The dining room, with its romantically set table, sat to the left of the front door, the living room to the right. While still in the foyer, I quickly looked behind me. On the opposite end of the foyer was the kitchen and I thought a back door. He guided me to the table and held out my chair, gesturing for me to sit. "You sit too, Laude," and pointed to a small pink plaid dog bed. We both did as we were told.

"I hope you like it. I've heard the food and service is excellent here." He smiled.

I wasn't sure if it was a joke or not, but felt it best to smile back.

"I figured every one likes Italian," and he handed me a menu. All day I had wondered how much he knew about me but he didn't know I didn't like eggplant. Eggplant parmigianania and chicken parmigiana were my two choices. The menu said it was a prix fixe including salad and dessert, but the price wasn't listed. I always thought it was a bad sign when a menu did not have prices listed; that couldn't have been more true than tonight.

"So, do you know what you'd like?," he asked politely.

I placed the menu down. "Chicken parmiginia, please."

"Great, me too! I'll let the kitchen know." He smirked and I had a strange feeling he knew about the eggplant. He went into the kitchen through the swinging door behind him.

I took a deep breath and looked around. The house didn't have the feel of a bachelor's pad. It looked like the home of a family. On the right wall was a large china cabinet, with fine china and crystal neatly arranged inside. The pattern resembled one Annie had considered choosing. I had spent an entire day with her while she selected items for her bridal registry. We stood for over an hour looking at dozens of patterns. I kept a smile on my face as she spent twenty minutes choosing between two contenders. I looked down at my place setting. The charger plate had an outer rim of cobalt blue and an inner rim of gold. The silverware was properly set, as was the crystal. Another thing I had learned with my outing with Annie.

I had never seen a man set a table like this before. I had never known a man that could. Anytime I had had a date at a man's house it was strictly paper and plastic. Either this wasn't his house, maybe the real owners' were in another cell in the basement, or he had lived here as part of a couple.

On the far wall, with the kitchen on the other side of it, there was a dark wood framed abstract painting, in different shades of blue. On the wall to the left, a large gold rimmed sunburst mirror. Behind me, there was a large window. The front door appeared to be the best exit. But, it had a dead bolt, which needed a key. Before I could get up to take a closer look, Craig came back in with the salads and what appeared to be water in crystal goblets. He placed the salads and water goblets down and sat across from me again. He raised his glass. "Cheers," he said.

I had closely checked the food and drinks before I ate anything from the bedroom closet earlier in the day. Nothing had appeared to be tampered with. The seals were intact on the water bottles and the peanut butter and jelly jars. I had made a peanut butter and jelly sandwich and drank a bottled water and nothing had me sick or drowsy. I had no way to check this food and drink. In attempts to keep with the plan to play along, I picked up my glass, clinked his waiting glass and took a small sip. Just water, I thought, I hoped.

"So tell me about yourself," he asked.

"What would you like to know?," I answered. I wanted to ask 'What don't you already know?'

He seemed to contemplate the question seriously and then asked "Favorite color?"

"Green."

"Of course, to match those pretty eyes." He looked at me intently but it didn't feel as creepy as it did last night. Surprising considering the situation.

We sat in silence as he ate his salad. I pushed mine around. Laude sat on her bed watching me.

"Aren't you hungry?" Before I could answer, he continued, "No, nervous right? Me too. First dates are like that."

I didn't correct him that it wasn't our first date.

He finished his salad. "Let's see how the kitchen's doing. I'm sure our entrees are ready." With our plates in hand, Craig entered the kitchen and I heard plates being scraped. I slowly got up to check the front door. Before I could take a step, a buzzer started to going off. Craig ran in, eyes wild. "What's going on? Where are you going?," he yelled.

Startled by the apparent alarm and his quick entrance, I blurted out "I just got up to pet Laude. What's that noise?" Laude had started howling from the high-pitched alarm. I picked her up and covered her ears.

He calmed down quickly. "Oh, sorry. Never mind. I'll reset it."

I remained standing and waited for him to shut it off and return to the kitchen.

He gestured to the chair. "Just sit down. Dinner's coming." It wasn't a request. I put Laude back on the bed and sat back down. The alarm stopped and he returned to the kitchen.

A few minutes later, he returned with our dinners. If I wasn't terrified, I would have been impressed. It could have been from a fancy Italian restaraunt- the golden brown chicken topped with sauce, bubbling cheese, and parsley. The twirled pasta lay next to it, with sauce, and lightly topped with parmesan.

I pushed the food around on my plate. I'd take a bite when he looked at me. He made no attempts at conversation. I'd catch him looking at me, as if he was going to speak. He'd smile awkwardly and return to his dinner.

At the conclusion of the dinner, he got Laude's leash and she followed him to the front door. She sat patiently as he hooked it. He took a keychain out of his pocket and unlocked the dead bolt. I watched from the window behind my chair as he paced back and forth. He was never out of my sight which also meant I was never out of his. He came back in, unleashed Laude and she ran for me. "Oh, I guess no treats tonight then Laude?"

Craig escorted us back down the stairs. "I'm so glad they matched us on 'Journey to Love'. I had a lovely time." I always felt awkward at the end of a date but nothing like this. He was acting as if he hadn't met me last night; as if he didn't know more than any first date should.

"May I call you again?," he asked nervously.

I didn't think I had a choice so I answered "If you'd like." What would he do if I said no? I didn't want to find out.

"Great! I'll call you." He sounded genuinely pleased. He waited until I opened the door and went in. Then I heard the dead bolt lock and his footsteps go up the stairs.

Unlike other dates I had been on, I knew when this date said he'd call, he would.

LILY

Sunday   February 15, 2009

Day one I had noticed all the similarities between the room I was in and my bedroom. Day two I noticed all the differences. To put it mildly, everything was just a little off.

The blue walls were a bit more blue. Aunt Florence and I had chosen the color together years ago, before I went to college. She said that since I was getting a new room, she needed a new room too. We picked the color "daydream," only partly based on the name. Years prior to that, we had chosen "beachball yellow" for her kitchen. The blaring headache producing yellow only lasted a week. We had quite a laugh and promised never to pick colors based on their name again, unless it was nail polish.

The trim and doors were a bright white here, they were "barely there" white at home. The furniture was positioned like mine. Next to the bed was the circular bedside table. Across from the bed and in the right corner, stood the dresser. The sleigh bed, nightstand and dresser, were cherry wood like mine but the curves were a little different. The comforter was the same pattern, white with a blue geometric pattern, but was newer. The material was crisper, as if it had just been purchased. The four pillows in white pillowcases were fluffier. The silver bedside lamp had one of those new energy conserving bulbs, instead of the standard three way bulb in mine.

Disturbingly though, one thing was exactly right. The Precious Moment figurine had the same chip on the edge. A pastel female figurine running towards a home plate and trunk with a wedding dress flowing out of it. My father had given it to me when I got accepted to college. I wasn't sure if it was a coincidence or if it was the one from my room.

When I took a shower, I found the same brand of shower gel, shampoo and conditioner that I had. I also found two marks on my right side that reminded me of vampire bites. They weren't in the right site for a vampire to get the most blood. Two small puncture marks, spaced an inch or two apart, on my right low back were surrounded by light bruising. Annie would have said I read too many supernatural novels. I guessed the marks were from a taser. From my limited knowledge of tasers, I assumed Craig must have used one on me in the elevator, since that was the last place I remembered being. I must have fallen, hitting my head, which left the small bruise on my left temple which I found while my hair was pulled back after the shower. I doubted that getting tasered and knocked out was what had kept me unconscious for over twelve hours; he had probably drugged my coffee as well. But it did explain the headache when I woke up and the knot above my left temple.

I looked closely at the marks, hoping not to see any signs of infection. There weren't any. The area looked clean which made me think a disinfectant had already been used. A shiver went down my spine as I realized Craig had had to undress me Friday night to put me into pajamas and had probably cleansed the area.

But that didn't answer how he got to the elevator before me. I wasn't surprised someone had let him in. Neighbors were always letting people in. But how did he get there before me? I left the coffee house before him. Damn Annie! I took a circuitous way home out of habit. She hadn't even reminded me to do it.

Surprisingly, Craig didn't "call" me on Sunday. But, he still called Laude for her walk three times.

LILY

Monday   February 16, 2009

Day three -- I thought help should be coming soon. Annie would be home from the wedding. She would have cell phone service again. She would try to call me and report me missing after hearing I wasn't at work. Franklin/Craig would be the obvious suspect. She'd tell the police about the date and give his information. The police would find his address and I'd be rescued. I watched the hours tick away and nothing happened. Then I realized it was President's Day. I had the day scheduled off of work. I had to work Christmas Eve and December 26th but somehow I got President's day off. Volume was low with school holidays so I got the day off. Somehow that job always screwed me.

I heard Craig leave after walking Laude in the morning. I had to pass another day in this strange room. My only entertainment was Laude and a clock radio. Laude only had one toy here, a purple octopus just like her favorite one at home.

Mid-day, I lied down to take a nap. I never took naps at home. I had slept fitfully the two previous nights and it was starting to catch up with me. The bed was comfortable but I tossed and turned. I finally willed myself to stay in one spot. I listened to the ocean waves that wafted through the walls. Most people would find it soothing but I thought it sounded artificial. It wasn't the light water crashing I heard from my open bedroom windows. I wondered if this sound machine had different options and if Craig would change it if I asked. The alternative might be worse, though. Silence would probably be best.

I resorted to counting sheep and it worked. I woke two hours later, not feeling refreshed. I was still lying on my back, on top of the covers. Laude was lying across my legs. She felt me stirring and looked up at me.

"Come here Laude," I said. She stretched and walked up next to me. I scratched her head for a few minutes and then she jumped off the bed and started running around. It was a little normalcy in an abnormal place.

Craig returned at five in the evening. He called Laude for her walk and I sat and waited for her return. I felt silly wondering why he hadn't 'called'. Laude returned and I gave her dinner.

At six, I heard an old fashioned telephone ring. I assumed it was coming from inside the house. I didn't have a phone in the bedroom, this one or my own. As I looked around, I realized it sounded like it was coming from the speaker. After the fourth ring, Craig said, through the speaker, "Aren't you home?"

I guessed this was his rendition of 'calling'. "Yes," I answered.

"Then answer the phone, silly."

I hadn't played make believe since I was four and hesitated on how to answer a phone that wasn't really ringing. "Hello?"

"Hi, it's Craig, from Saturday night. How are you?"

"Fine, thank you. Yourself?"

"Fine, thank you." There was silence. I had never been good with small talk on the phone with a date.

"So what did you do today?"

"Nothing much. Played with Laude."

"No work?"

"No, had the day off for President's Day."

"Oh, how nice. Didn't you read anything? I thought you read a lot. Your profile said you read avidly."

"I do. But I don't have any books."

"Why not?," he asked seriously. He was quite aware why I didn't have any books. He hadn't put any in the room.

This was stretching my ability to play make believe, so I said the truth. "I haven't been able to get to the library."

He paused, as if thinking about it, "Oh, maybe I could help you with that."

My response, "Thanks", was greeted with more silence.

"I'm pretty busy this week. Started a new job. Maybe we could get together Friday? Are you free?"

I wouldn't say I was free. "Yes." Again, I was sticking with my strategy of playing along.

"Ok, great. I'll pick you up at six."

LILY

Tuesday   February 17, 2009

I woke up after another night of broken sleep. Several books lay on my side of the dog door. Five of the six books were from authors I knew and enjoyed. One was from one I didn't know. I had already read one of the books. I guess he didn't know everything about me.

The question remained- How much did he know? And the things he knew, how did he learn them? I knew Annie didn't post pictures of my bedroom on my profile. She wouldn't have put on there that I ate peanut butter and jelly sandwich for lunch every day. I would have put that on there if I had done my own profile but she would have objected thinking it made me sound weird. I thought it made me sound reliable.

Craig had decorated a room to the basic dimensions of my room, almost an exact copy. Did he use binoculars from one of the apartments on the other end of my street to look in? But, how did he know which apartment was mine? Maybe after following me home, he saw me on the patio. I did tend to spend a lot of time out there and Laude drew attention to us with her barking at dogs passing by on the street.

But there was a level of detail that I didn't think binoculars could get. Annie, Susie and the building's superintendent, Tony, were the only ones who had keys. Annie certainly wasn't involved. Susie had been walking dogs in the building for years and had a good reputation. She wouldn't give my key to anyone. She would have told me if she had lost the key. She kept all of her keys in her fanny pack at all times. I had seen how carefully arranged her key ring was and she had told me how she had a coding system. Each key was labeled but not with the owner's address or the dogs name. Even if she had lost a key, no one but her would know which key was for what apartment.

Tony, the super, had worked in the building almost as long as Aunt Florence had lived there. He was a nice guy, conscientious about his work. There was no way he was involved. He was careful with keys too. I had seen how he kept the apartment keys in a locked cabinet in his office. The cabinet's key was always on his work belt.

When I saw the items in my pantry stocked with the items I bought, I thought maybe Craig had just followed me around a grocery store and followed me home. But that wouldn't explain the replication of the bedroom.

All I knew for sure was that 'Journey to Love' was involved. But what had happened first? Did he start to stalk me after seeing my profile or did he stalk me and found out I was on the dating site? But, I never spoke about being on the site. I didn't even complete my own profile. No one knew except Annie.

I had a lot of questions, and it was looking like I had a lot of time on my hands to find the answers.

LILY

Wednesday   February 18, 2009

I was starting to go stir crazy. I had read two books, listened to the radio. I tried to work out, running in place, jumping jacks, crunches, push-ups, but that only lasted ten minutes. I tracked the day by Laude's morning walk with Craig, breakfast, lunch, Laude's after work walk with Craig, dinner, Laude's night walk with Craig and then bed. He never spoke to me when he got Laude. She would hear the latch unlock and would bounce through the doggie door and up the stairs. I had no view of the outside and no idea if it was night or day. The bedside clock was the only way I could keep track of time; the radio personalities the only way I could keep track of the day and the outside world.

I changed to the 'all news, all the time' station but tired of it quickly. The talk of the ailing economy, the cold weather, and lack of talk of a missing Long Beach woman and her dog caused me to return to ESPN radio. The monotomy of the men talking about spring training and basketball droned on as I stared at the ceiling.

I got off the bed and took a closer look at the items in the dresser. There were fourteen pairs of socks, seven white, seven of mixed colors. There were fourteen panties and fourteen bras. As with the dress and shoes, they were the right size. I wasn't surprised by the panties. Anyone could take a good guess that I was a size small. I was surprised by the bras. I had dated men that couldn't have told you my bra size. In a crude way, they could have told a salesperson my cup size but not the band size. I had a pit in my stomach when I thought that maybe Craig had been in my apartment, literally going through my drawers. I remembered shopping a few weeks ago and buying underwear. It was disturbing that I was relieved that I had been stalked instead of a stranger had been in my apartment.

The theme of fourteen continued. Another drawer had five t-shirts, five long sleeve shirts and four tank tops. The next drawer had five pairs of jeans, five sweatpants, four pairs of shorts. I pulled out the shorts and held them up. It was the middle of winter, when was I going to be wearing shorts? Of course, I had no idea when I'd get out of this room again so the question was moot.

The last drawer had pajamas. Two sets were short sleeved and two long sleeved. Except for the date, when I wore the dress, I had worn pajamas. I didn't think Annie would have hassled me about it.

Tears welled in my eyes at the thought of her. I tried to picture her and Harry. It was midday. Harry was probably napping. Annie was most likely doing housework or thinking about what to make Jeffrey and her for dinner or maybe having a cup of tea while she watched a talk show. I went into the bathroom and closed the bathroom door. Laude squeezed in before it closed.

The dress I had worn on the date with Craig hung on the hook on the door. I thought of the outfit Annie had told me to wear for the date with Franklin. It was nowhere in the room. The shoes weren't either. The only pair of shoes I had here were the black heels. Not exactly escaping shoes. Maybe he had thought of that; that I wouldn't try to run without shoes in the freezing temperatures. I think the possibility of frost bite was the least of my problems.

I took a tissue and dabbed the tears from my eyes. Thoughts of Annie and Harry during a normal day had started the crying. They couldn't possibly have normalcy while I was missing. She had to be looking for me.

I looked into the mirror and stared at myself. I saw a pale girl with green eyes looking back. My hair was curly, not frizzy today. I guess being locked up had one positive—no humidity. I wondered what Craig saw when he looked at me. Did he see me or someone else? Someone he wanted me to be? Was he going to mold me into his perfect woman? Or had he seen me as easy prey? A young woman who lived alone, with the added bonus of no family. Or did he see me? I wasn't sure if it mattered. What mattered is that I needed to survive long enough to be rescued.

Why hadn't Annie found me yet? Franklin was the obvious suspect. I looked around and knew this had been well planned. Disguising himself on 'Journey to Love' had to be part of it. That could be the only reason for the delay.

In a perverse way, I felt better after going through the drawers. If he had been through my apartment, he would not have found the drawers organized. Nothing was folded in my closets or drawers.

The problem was the reoccurring fourteen. Did I only have fourteen days? Or did he know I did laundry every two weeks? I doubted I would get a field trip to a laundromat. I shivered at the thought of Craig washing my undergarments and made a mental note to hand wash some tomorrow.

At seven in the evening, the telephone rang from the walls. I answered, "Hello."

"How are you?," he asked.

"Good, thanks."

"Really, you look a little bored this evening. No reading?"

Well, that answered another question. He had video on me as well as sound. I wasn't surprised but it did creep me out. There was a pause as I processed that and he realized his error.

"I was calling to confirm Friday."

"Ok, what time?"

"Seven good for you?"

"Sure, see you then," and I hung up. Well, as best as I could in this land of make believe.

LILY

Thursday   February 19, 2009

I woke up to find more books at the doggie door but the rest of the day was the same.

I thought back about Craig's admission that he could see me. I figured the camera was in the speaker and tried to avoid it. I would start to dress in the bathroom and hope there was no camera in there.

I assumed that every day he went to work. After Laude's morning walk, I heard a car leave and it would return around five. I couldn't imagine what type of job it was but I imagined his co-workers would describe him as being nice, but aloof. They'd be surprised by his crime of kidnapping but not shocked. I doubted he could watch me continuously. Could he check on the video feed mid-day? Could he watch the day's events when he got home? Was that his idea of entertainment?

I was hoping my days were numbered here, but, please God, not numbered in general. It would be a good idea to learn as much as I could in case the cavalry didn't come.

LILY

Friday   February 20, 2009

Before I could worry about what to wear for our second "date," I woke to find another box at the doggie door. It contained my outfit. Skinny jeans in dark denim, calf high brown leather boots, and a pink cashmere sweater. His taste wasn't exactly the same as mine but it was good, and certainly not inexpensive. The labels were from stores I had heard of but had never shopped in. Again it was all in my size and all fit well. I was dressed and as ready as I could be when I heard him walk down the stairs to my door.

The pattern of the date was the same as last time. Craig knocked, I asked who was there, he answered and unlocked us from our cell. As he stood outside the door, I took a good look at him. Our first meeting at the coffee house I had only noticed the crazy eyes. Our first "date" here, I was too dazed to register much about him. I was focused on getting away from him.

Tonight I took a good look at him. If I had seen him out on the street with a date, I would have thought she was a lucky girl. He was good looking in a grey dress shirt, untucked, and jeans. His eyes were a handsome grey-ish blue. Instead of looking crazy, they looked thoughtful. His hair was lightly tousled, flatter on his head.

He escorted Laude and I upstairs and into the dining room which was, once again, set for two. I could feel the adrenaline coursing through my veins. My palms were sweaty. I felt like I did on other second dates. Not sure if I should have accepted, if I should I reach for the check. The anxiety feeling was the same but the reasons significantly different.

He instructed both of us to sit in our respective seats. We both obeyed- Laude to her dog bed; me to the dining chair with my back to the large bay window. After settling into his own chair, he reported "I already ordered for us. I hope that is alright."

"Sure."

"How do you like your steak?"

I hesitated. Saying rare would make the evening end quicker; saying well would take longer in the kitchen, hopefully occupying him. "Well, thank you."

"Great, cheers," he held out his glass. It appeared to be water, again. His knowledge of me extended to my avoidance of alcohol.

"Cheers." I clinked our glasses together.

"Well, let me check on our meal," and he got up to go into the kitchen.

Once the swinging door closed behind him, I slowly counted to five and called Laude over to me. I hoped to get a quick look at the front door, if it was unlocked I'd run.

I picked Laude up, put her on the chair as I slid off of it to evade activating the alarm. But the moment I left the seat, the alarm sounded. I guess a ten pound Laude wasn't enough weight. The chair alarm was able to register the hundred pound difference.

Again, Craig came running into the room, screaming "What's wrong? Where are you going?" With Laude in my arms, I tried to calm him down, again telling him I just wanted to get Laude. That reassured him and he went back to the kitchen once the both of us had sat back down in our respective spots.

Dinner seemed to be taking longer than I would expect. I suppressed a laugh at the thought of complaining to management. It seemed quiet in the kitchen. Without shifting my weight too much, I felt around the bottom of the chair in hopes of finding the wires to the alarm to no avail. I started looking around the room for something that I could put on my seat and not set off the alarm. Nothing seemed appropriate. I heard Craig in the kitchen and stopped moving around.

Craig came back into the dining room with our dinners, T-bone steaks, baked potatoes, broccoli. It was all prepared just the way I liked it: the steak well done, the baked potato lightly buttered, the broccoli steamed.

The dinner itself was uneventful. The food was good, the best I had eaten in over a week, probably longer. I held myself back from devouring it. The conversation normal, despite the circumstances. A few brief and uncomfortable exchanges about the weather and other trivial items nobody cared about. I told him about the book I just read. He told me about his new job.

"What do you do?," I asked.

"I work with computers."

I nodded, thinking the answer was vague, but not knowing enough to ask a followup.

"I told you I work on designing computer software programs."

"Sorry, I didn't remember," I shrugged.

"You asked it in your first email. How do you not remember that?," he asked, watching me closely.

I regretted not reviewing his profile; not reviewing my own. I had no idea what Annie had put on mine. Had she put an accurate profile of me? Or what she wanted me to be?

His jaw was set and I feared his anger if he found out it wasn't me he had emailed. "Just nervous. Forgot. Sorry."

"Come on. How could you forget I work with computers?" His expression was neutral and I wasn't sure if he was being playful or was on the verge of anger. "How else can you explain that I was the only one who responded to your profile?"

"What?," I responded. He was the only who responded to the profile? It explained Annie's eagerness that I like him.

"Oh no. You didn't know!" He smiled weakly.

Tears welled in my eyes as I realized his extensive knowledge of computer programming, proved by having hacked into the 'Journey to Love' website. He would be untraceable. Fortunately, he misread my tears.

"I'm so sorry. I didn't realized that might hurt your feelings."

With a lull in the conversation and our meals finished, I thought it was a good time to tell him.

"Craig, this has been very nice. But, I'd like to go home now. Please."

"Oh, no dessert?"

"No, thank you. I think it's time Laude and I went home." At the sound of her name, Laude jumped up and ran over to me. I picked her up and stood from the chair. Craig came over and turned off the alarm.

He looked at me intently. "Ok, well, I had a nice time. Let's go."

I headed to the front door, as I got closer I knew it was too good to be true. I put my hand on the doorknob and my heart started to race as it began to turn. Then I felt his hand lightly grab my arm.

"Lillian, you're so silly. That's not your door. Your door is to the right." He sounded like he was laughing. I was afraid to look at him, not knowing what I'd find, but knew there was no choice. I turned to face him and he was genuinely smiling.

Holding Laude close, I looked him straight in the eyes. Eyes that I had first seen as crazy, but had since seen something else. I had seen glimpses of a handsome man. A funny and smart man like the one Annie had described. The crazed look was back and I was scared. My heart pounded in my chest as I waited to see what he would say and do.

"Please, Craig. I would like to go home. It has been a week. People miss me."

He paused and then laughed heartily. "You'd be surprised how many people miss *you*." Before I could respond, he increased his grip on my arm, pushing me in the direction of the basement stairs. He swung the basement door open, with more force than was necessary, and kept a firm grip on my arm down the stairs and back into the bedroom. As he nudged me in, he looked me directly in the eyes and politely said, "This is your home now."

I stood inches from the door as he gently closed it and locked it. I remained there, staring at the door for five minutes, not knowing what to do. I listened as he walked back up the stairs, closed the basement door, and locked it. I wasn't sure which comment was more upsetting- about people missing me or that this was my home. I sat down against the wall realizing there was nothing left to do but cry.

After several minutes, Laude started licking my face and I stopped sobbing. Crying was something she had grown accustomed to, although its frequency and intensity had decreased over the past few months. She had learned that jumping on my lap and licking my face made it stop. It also brought a treat, most likely her motivation.

I looked around "my" room and thought about what he had said. I knew this wasn't my home but he clearly thought it was and had no intentions of letting me leave. His intentions shouldn't have surprised me but hearing them was shocking nonetheless.

"You'd be surprised how many people miss you." I would be surprised if large manhunts were organized. I'd be surprised to see milk cartons with my picture being sold. I didn't think that was what he meant. He sounded relieved when he said it. He couldn't say it without laughing. He didn't sound anxious. That could only mean one thing.

I'd be surprised because no one missed me.

LILY

Saturday   February 21, 2009

I woke up at eight, according to the bedside clock. For a few glorious moments, I thought I was in my own bed, in my own room. I was jarred into reality by the metallic click of the doggie door lock and Laude jumping of the bed.

I relived the last week. Waking up into an alternative universe, this weird replica of my bedroom and my life, meeting 'Craig', and our dates. I laughed that Annie would be so happy that I had had three dates in just over a week.

Where was Annie? Certainly she missed me and was looking for me. Even if she thought I was so furious that I didn't want to speak to her, she would have known something was wrong when I didn't show up for work for a week. I was thankful I had changed my emergency contact information at work in September to Annie. It was originally Aunt Florence. But with months of no contact I felt it best to change it to Annie. I knew Aunt Florence wouldn't care.

The reality was it was foolish to have wasted a week passively waiting for help.

Craig was a smart man who had planned this well. It had been naive to think that I should just wait. Even if Annie suspected 'Franklin', his profile would be untraceable. It was unlikely she would suspect him anyway since I was already in my building when I had called her. The staff at Roasters would probably not be helpful either. I'd be surprised if they took any notice of an average couple. If they had any video surveillance, it was probably directed at the cash register. Even if they had taken notice of us, they wouldn't provide an accurate physical description of him. He had appeared taller and bulkier that first night. The slicked back hair significantly changed his look. I'm sure it was all part of his plan.

Week one I was in shock. I had waited for rescue. I asked to leave. I learned no help was coming.

Week two I would try to figure out how to get out.

LILY

Sunday   February 22, 2009

Laude had adapted to our new situation very well. She heard Craig come down the steps and she ran through the doggie door the moment she heard it unlock. I didn't bother to get out of bed. I knew he'd bring her back in fifteen minutes.

On schedule, I heard them come down the stairs and Laude ran back in. She was excited from her morning walk and wanted breakfast. After rubbing her ears, I rolled out of bed to get it. While in the pantry, I noticed it had been re-stocked. I considered when he could have done this. The only option was when he was cooking dinner on Friday and remembered that it took longer than I expected. Laude, frustrated by my slowness, started barking. I filled her bowl and she ate eagerly. I sadly realized that neither of us ate yesterday and I had never gone into the pantry. In a room with no natural light, I had found it too easy to stay in bed and pull the covers over my head after another investigation for an escape was unsuccessful.

The unlocking of the doggie door stirred me from the pantry. Craig dropped a familiar white box through. I picked it up not needing to read the blue lettering to know what it was or where it was from. It was a Rein's box, my bakery. The bakery I visited every Sunday, with Aunt Florence and without her. I wasn't surprised he knew I had frequented the bakery. It was the closest one to my home.

I heard my stomach growl and opened the box. I found a cheese danish, a Russian tea biscuit, a raspberry glazed donut and a cruller. In a well stocked bakery, with many breakfast items, this was no coincidence.

I knew a little more. He had followed me at least four Sundays.

LILY

Monday   February 23, 2009

I heard him leave for work and knew I had about eight hours.

I looked at the "window." It was the most obvious means of escape. I was in a basement and knew there wasn't a window of the same size behind it. Typically there were small windows in a basement. I knew Laude was small enough to fit through. I thought I was small enough, too. I had kept the shade down to keep the awful picture covered. I raised it now to take a closer look at the plywood. I banged on it and it barely moved. I took one of the hard covered books and banged it against it. It didn't even dent it.

I considered pulling the nails out but they were in firmly. I knew the plastic knife would be useless but I tried it anyway. The results were as expected.

During my next date, I would have to smuggle silverware out.

I considered my other options. The room looked newly built. I knocked on the walls to find the studs.

I thought of my apartment. The one I never wanted, the one I never dreamed would be mine. Would I go into arrears and lose it if the managing agent didn't get the maintenance fee on the first of the month? I had always paid on time and didn't know the late policy. Would Annie be able to pay it?

I shook myself out of it. That wasn't important right now. Did I really like living there anyway? I had started planning my departure a couple weeks ago.

I returned to looking for the studs. I kept knocking on the wall with the dresser against it but everything sounded solid. I moved the dresser from the wall, trying not to disturb the speaker. I took one of the hard cover books and hit the wall with it. No damage. No magical light showing daylight. Based on my limited knowledge of the layout of the upstairs, I had assumed the wall with the "window" was against the side of the house. Knocking on the wall there sounded the same as the wall the dresser was against. I assumed both were concrete and I couldn't punch my way out. Sit-coms always made punching through a wall look so easy. So did the home improvement shows. But those men usually had some large tool to break down the walls.

I had a flashback to 'Shawshank Redemption.' The lead character, Andy, had used some small tool to tunnel out of the prison. That had been through concrete. If I got some small tool or knife I could try it.

I just hoped I hadn't been served a life sentence, like Andy.

LILY

Wednesday   February 25, 2009

There was a knock at the door. I had heard him coming down the stairs so it wasn't unexpected. What happened next was.

He opened the door before I could answer. Fortunately I was dressed. He seemed pleased.

"It's an anniversary of sorts," he grinned. "I was in the area so I thought I'd see if you were available." If any date had ever showed up at my door unannounced, I would have found it unsettling. This only reinforced my opinion. Annie would have said it was romantic.

I wasn't sure what anniversary it was and debated whether or not to ask. I remembered a quote- something about knowledge is power and asked, "What anniversary is it?"

"Nothing you'd remember, Lillian." I translated that to mean when the stalking started.

I climbed the stairs and noticed I was slightly out of breath. It startled me that just one flight of stairs could be that taxing. In the past twelve days, I had limited activity. Initially I had worked out but that had only lasted a day or two.

Craig escorted us into the living room instead of the dining room. It was the same size and shape of the dining room, also with a swinging door which I assumed went into the kitchen. Two ivory couches, with light blue striping, faced each other with a glass coffee table in between. Several framed floral prints hung from the caramel colored walls.

I glimpsed out the large bay window. There was only darkness. I could make out a few trees but no lights from neighboring homes or traffic.

Like the dining room, it had a woman's touch. Again, I had the feeling that a woman had lived here. It felt modern. A younger woman had lived here, not an older woman. I didn't think this was his mother's home; maybe he had lived here with a wife. Maybe he had hired a decorator, but it didn't feel professionally designed.

Two tea cups and a plate of cookies sat on the coffee table. I scolded Laude when she put her paws on the table and sniffed at the cookies. Her ears perked up and she looked at me. I told her to get down. She did, stealing a cookie before doing so. She ran off behind the couch. I got up to snatch the cookie away.

Craig laughed and said, "Don't worry. There's no chocolate in them." We both laughed when Laude came back, licking her chops, and sat at my feet. "I hope you like the cookies as much as she did!" I looked down at her and she looked very pleased with herself.

"I love to see you laugh," he said smiling. The smile faded and he added, "I hate to see you cry." I wondered if it was a veiled threat. I'd cried often in that room, a room he closely monitored. He continued before I could get worried. "We've both had loss. Loss is hard but we have each other now. It'll be better."

I looked down at my tea cup to avoid his intense stare. I knew what my own loss was but wondered what his was.

When we finished our tea, he took Laude out the front door. He was always in view through the bay window. We both knew I would try nothing when he had Laude.

When they returned, he took her leash off and asked, "Treat?" She sat and raised her paw to shake. He handed her the treat and patted her on the head. "Good girl, Laude. You sure are one smart pup. You learned to do that in just a few days."

He was watching Laude while he said it and never saw my shocked face when I realized that was where she learned to shake hands. If Susie had met a stranger on the street who taught her a trick, she would have written a detailed note about it. She told me about every new 'friend' she made during their walks so this would have been big news.

In that one move, many questions were answered. He'd been in my home, several times.

The more I learned the more surprised I was. I knew Craig had watched me for over four weeks. I knew he had taken a close look at my bedroom. I liked believing he had done it through binoculars, from a block away. Correction, I didn't like the thought that a stranger had used binoculars to spy on me but it was better than the alternative, that he had been in my home. I couldn't fathom any way he could have gotten in but it didn't matter what I thought possible, what I wanted to believe. He had been in my apartment. And not just once.

Some watchdog Laude had turned out to be.

He returned us to our prison/bedroom to find a television and cable box on the dresser with a big red bow. I had no idea how and when he had done this. It was probably when I asked for more hot water for my tea. I was surprised when he got up and asked Laude to follow him. I was more surprised when she did. I had used the time to steal a spoon and then to decide where to hide it.

Attached to the bow was a card -
Happy Anniversary.
Spring training game tomorrow 1:10 p.m.
Love, Craig.

I laughed when I sarcastically asked myself "How did he know?" Considering I wore a Mets jacket practically every day, it wasn't too difficult to conclude my allegiance. Annie had given me strict instructions not to wear one of them on the date. I laughed again when I tried to remember what anniversary was electronics. I stopped when I realized there may be more anniversaries spent here.

LILY

Thursday   February 26, 2009

The first thing I had done the night before was put on the television when I got 'home.' The channels were the same so I assumed I was still on Long Island. I put on the local news channel. Every half hour they broadcasted the news, with the emphasis on Long Island. There were no reports of me missing, not even on the scrolling bottom line. I knew I shouldn't be surprised but I was. Having run out of options to find Franklin, I hoped to see Annie on the television pleading to find me. Craig's words -"You'd be surprised how many people miss you."- rang in my head.

At noon, I put on SNY, the Mets channel. This was the first positive part of my current predicament. I could watch baseball in the middle of a weekday, live. I had never watched much spring training baseball. Dad had told me there was no point getting too excited or too dejected about spring training results because they were forgotten on Opening Day. Still, I approached the game like it was the World Series.

When the game started, I closed my eyes and listened to the announcers, Gary, Keith and Ron. It was a beautiful sunny day in Port St. Lucie, Florida. I pictured myself there- the sun on my face, the smell of spring in the air. I put out of my mind my unsuccessful escape attempts earlier in the day.

After I heard Craig leave for the day, I put the spoon I had stolen the night before to use. To little use that is. Not surprisingly, a spoon had little effect on the nails on the plywood over the 'window' or on the wall behind the bed. With no posters in the room to hide any progress, I had decided behind the bed would be the safest bet.

Next time, I had to steal a knife.

LILY

Friday February 27, 2009

I had woken to the familiar click of the doggie door and Laude running for it. I had hoped Craig would "call" last night to arrange another date. I pulled the covers over my head and rebuked myself that I was disappointed when my kidnapper/stalker/madman hadn't wanted to talk to me. I was bored and lonely and he was the only human contact I had.

I spent the day watching television, mostly mindless drivel, and watching another Mets spring training game. I held back tears thinking about Dad. We always planned to go to St. Lucie but never got there. Every year, we said we'd do it next year. Neither of us ever thought that there wouldn't be a next year. If he was still alive, they would have found me by now. I couldn't know that for sure but at least I'd know someone would be looking. Mom and Dad would have given desperate pleas for my safe return on television. Maybe it was better that they didn't live to see this.

After the game, I flipped back to the local news station. Still nothing. I rolled over, burying my face in the pillow, trying to muffle my sobs. How could Annie not miss me? How could she not be doing something to find me? I'd been gone two weeks!

Laude pawed at my arm. I wiped tears away and then petted her behind her ear. "Laude, I'm surprised no one from the condo is making pleas to find you. Or Susie." She looked at me and tilted her head from side to side in agreement.

"Good evening, Lillian." His voice through the walls startled me even though I knew he was home. He had already walked Laude. Thankfully, he had put aside the pretense of the phone ringing.

"Thank you for the television."

"You're welcome. I didn't want you to miss the Mets games."

I debated the next sentence over the past few days. The wave sounds were driving me insane. It was ironic that the sound I had always loved was now grating my last nerve. The question was do I come out and ask him to turn it off or do I coyly mention that I found it disturbing. 'Please Craig shut off the sound machine' or, to keep up the ruse that I was truly in my own home, 'The waves are disturbingly loud the last few days.' and hope he got the hint.

I had learned the hard way that most men don't take hints well but Craig wasn't most men. He was far more perceptive than anyone else I had ever dated. I had shuddered earlier in the day when that thought went through my head. I had finally decided it was best to try to keep up appearances. Craig had been nice so far and who knows what he'd do if I upset his reality.

"The waves are real strong the last few days. I really had to turn up the volume to hear the game."

He laughed, "Ok, Lillian."

I had the disturbing vision of him shaking his head in disbelief like Annie would when I said something ridiculous.

"I'm sorry for the late notice. I meant to ask you Wednesday but I was so distracted by getting the television set up but would you like to go out tomorrow?"

"I'd love to." And that was the truth.

Seconds later, the ocean sound was gone.

NATHAN

Friday   6:20 p.m.   February 27, 2009   Long Beach, NY

"What are you doing here, Nathan? I'm sorry. *Detective Miccoli.*"

"And don't you forget it!" I answered. Steve walked from the open building door to shake my hand. Each time I saw him I thought he'd put on more weight. His uniform looked more snug than the time before. At five and a half feet, extra pounds showed quickly on him. "You know it's not official yet, though." I had been promoted to detective a few weeks ago but was still waiting for my assignment.

"I thought we were meeting at my place," Steve said. He ran his hand through his receding black hair. I thought the closely cropped cut drew more attention to its thinning and made him look older than his thirty years. Self-consciously, I ran my hand through my brown hair, thankful it was all still there. The increasing number of gray I saw in the mirror never bothered me when I thought of Steve.

He signaled for me to follow him and we walked through the apartment building's elevator. "Ya, I know," I answered. "But I saw your patrol car when I was driving by and thought I'd find out why you were running late."

"Sorry. Girl missing. Strike that. Twenty four year old woman." Steve had been forced to work on his political correctness after a complaint from a female co-worker. "Her friend has called the department over six times in the last two days so *the chief* sent me over."

Former chief was his Uncle Bobby. The current Chief Sonja and Steve didn't see eye to eye. Steve didn't see eye to eye with too many people, literally and figuratively.

As we stepped off the elevator on the fifth floor, he continued. "I already looked around the apartment. Found nothing. Just have to go back in for a second. I left the Missing Persons Report in there."

"How long she been gone?," I asked. As he entered the apartment, I stood in the doorway. I looked around the simple apartment. It looked barely lived in. There was nothing hung on the walls; no personal touches anywhere in sight.

"Two weeks," Steve answered.

I shook my head in disbelief. "That's a long time."

"Well, we don't know if she's missing, or left, or..."

"What do you mean?" I looked at Steve, not knowing where he was going with this.

"We got a call from a lady last week rambling on and on about a missing dog. She's a dog walker; dog's gone. She's distraught. I give her the number for the shelter. Tell her to call local vets, post signs, whatever. I figure she lost the dog and knows the owner is going to be pissed. But, she says the owner's gone too. I look up the girl's name, no missing person report. I tell the woman sorry she's lost a client but not a police matter. She just wouldn't stop about the damn dog. Then we get a call from an out of state friend who says she can't reach the lady either and files the report." Steve walked around the apartment, continuing to gesture wildly. "She lives close to where we used to. Ardsley, Pennsylvania."

Steve left the apartment and headed back to the elevator. "Steve, aren't you going to lock the place up?"

"Don't worry. The super let me in. He'll lock up."

I followed him back to the elevator, again shaking my head. "So, for two weeks, no one knew she was gone?"

"Not anyone who reported it."

"Case gonna be a little cold."
"What case? Maybe she's just gone. The more her friend rattled on, the more I realized she probably just left."

I returned to my car while Steve went to look for the super, after I reminded him to do it. Something intrigued me about the case. When Steve came out of the building, Missing Persons Report in his hand, I walked over to his patrol car. He started talking to one of the residents. I put my hand out asking for the report without interrupting him. I assumed he was questioning the neighbor about the missing woman but then I heard him say "Yankees" and knew his attention had already strayed from the case.

I scanned the two page report. Her friend, Annie, had certainly put a lot of detail into it, and a rather odd photo. As I completed reading it, Steve's attention shifted back to me as the resident entered the building. I handed the report back to him.

Waving the report in his hand, "That woman got this off the internet. Can you believe that?" Shaking his head, he looked up from the paperwork, "Who does that?"

"Someone who wants Genevieve Lillian Brannon found."

I waited in the police department's parking lot as Steve finished up his work day and changed out of his uniform. When he lumbered out the door, I got out of my car, preparing for our monthly routine.

"Where do you want to go for dinner?," Steve asked as he approached me.

"Doesn't matter to me. Your town, your choice."

The conversation was always the same, and the final destination was always the same. Sammie's in the West End. We always placed the same order, too.

"Sammie's it is. Just follow me," Steve answered.

The days leading up to a dinner, I often contemplated canceling. We no longer had much in common. My conscience never let me. Steve and I had been best friends in grammar school together in Willow Grove, Pennsylvania. We kept in touch after he moved to Long Island after his parents' divorce during the seventh grade. When I moved to New York for college it was nice to know someone else in the area. At different colleges, we both studied criminal justice. He followed his uncle's footsteps at the Long Beach Police Department and I went to the New York Police Department.

We sat down at a table. I grinned, thankful we didn't sit at the same table every time.

"How's Mom?," Steve asked. It always unnerved me when he called my mother 'mom'. He always viewed her as the perfect mother. She was a mother who was home when the kids got off the school bus waiting with a snack, unlike his own who was never home after school. He hadn't started calling her 'Mom' until college. I didn't know what my mother would say if she knew.

"Fine, thanks. She's starting to date. Frightening concept. Glad I'm not there to witness that." Dad died two years ago, but it was still odd to think about my mom going out on a date. "But, I'm going Saturday to stay a few days."

"Tell her I said hello. Speaking of dating, you seeing anyone?"

"No one consistently." Even if I were, I would have told him no. I learned in college not to bring girlfriends around Steve. He meant well but while trying to tell a girl my attributes he'd slide into yesteryear. Few girls wanted to hear how my first kiss was with his cousin or about our little league prowess. "How's Katie? Date set yet?," I asked to divert him from follow up questions.

"Katie's good. I'll let you know, *best man*, when she lets me know." A shiver went through me at the thought of arranging and attending his bachelor party.

NATHAN

Saturday   11:30 a.m.   February 28, 2009   Willow Grove, PA

As I pulled up to the house, it was hard to believe Mom hadn't sold it. She didn't need the four bedroom home she had raised her three children in anymore. But two years after my dad died, she was still there and nothing much had changed.

I yelled, "Hi, Mom," as I entered my childhood home.

"Nathan, I thought you were getting here for dinner." She came out of the kitchen, wiping her hands on a dishtowel.

"Got an early start, thought you'd be glad to see me." Of course she was and gave me a big hug and kiss. As she stepped away, I noticed she was dressed up for a Saturday afternoon. She looked a little guilty, too.

"I have plans this afternoon. I'm sorry." She paused, while ringing her hands. "I'll cancel. What am I thinking? My gorgeous and favorite son is home." She gave me another hug and walked back into the kitchen. "Hungry? I'll make you lunch."

Feeling guilty that I had disturbed her plans, I assured her, "No, Mom. Go out. I'll be fine. I don't want to mess up your day. Thought I'd hit less traffic leaving early." I could see she was debating whether to leave or not. "Go, Go. I promise not to get into trouble." I got the response I had gotten countless times as a teenager, raised eyebrows and a knowing look. "Not too much anyway," and gave her the smile that always made her smile back and had gotten me out of answering too many questions. Almost always.

"Ok, I won't be long. Just brunch and then I'll make your favorites!"

With a few hours to waste, I thought I'd drive around and see what had changed since my last visit in December. Before I realized what I was doing, I was in front of Mrs. Annie Follette's house.

It was a sunny day, warm for February. A young woman and a little boy were playing in the front yard. His blue knit hat lay on the ground twenty feet away. His dark hair splayed in all directions. His mother went and picked the hat up. The little one watched her and then took off once she had it in her hands. For a little guy, probably about a year old, he gave her a bit of a race, for a few feet.

I probably should have stayed in the car and driven back to Willow Grove. Maybe my old high school team was having a spring practice. Maybe mom was back from her "date."

An overwhelming part of me wanted to know how this woman could have so many details about Ms. Brannon but not notice or, maybe not care, that she had been gone for two weeks.

As I walked towards her, I knew I had caught her off guard. I didn't know who she thought I was but it wasn't someone good. I had been told more than once that even out of uniform I looked like a cop. Annie obviously agreed.

"Oh, my god! Please no!" She fell to her knees and covered her face. The little boy ran to his mother and started crying, too. Maybe coming had been a mistake.

"Mrs. Follette. Calm down." I squatted next to her and patted her on her arm. Calming down victims and witnesses had never been my strong suit. With two sisters and a mother, you would think I could handle a crying woman better. I looked around to see if any neighbors had taken notice. A stranger hovering over a young mother in this neighborhood would definitely be noticed. Mrs. Follette and her son appeared to be the only two enjoying this almost spring day, until I arrived.

Tears rolling down her face, she looked up at me. "You found her. And not in a good way." She buried her head in her hands again. "Oh Lily, oh my god, Lily. What am I going to do without you?"

"It's alright, Mrs Follette. I just came to talk to you about Ms. Brannon. I learned of the missing persons report from a friend who works on the Long Beach Police Department and my mom lives a few miles away. I just wanted to talk to you."

She seemed to calm down, which quickly calmed the little boy down, too.

"Why don't we go inside, ma'am." She took my hand to stand and the little boy took hers and I followed them into the house. She smoothed her hair back and readjusted her dark hair in her ponytail.

"I'm so sorry. It's just...," She wiped the tears from her face and then reached down and did the same for the boy. "Please call me Annie. This is Harry." I followed them into the house through the dining room into the kitchen where she got Harry something to drink.

"Please sit." She pointed to the chair across from the large window looking into the backyard. As Harry got older and maybe other children arrived, Annie would enjoy looking out the window to watch them play. My mom had a similar one in her home and she loved cooking dinner and watching her three children playing in the yard throughout the years.

"Would you like some coffee?" I shook my head no. "Anything to drink?" Mrs. Follette, Annie, had recovered quickly from her initial scare of my arrival and what she thought it meant.

She sat down across from me and Harry ran over to her with arms extended. She picked him up and placed him on her lap. She flattened his hair down and swept it out of his eyes.

"I'm Detective Miccoli. Nathan. NYPD." Annie nodded and waited for more. I knew I shouldn't have told her 'Detective'. I hadn't started my detective training or position yet. Before I could start what I had come for, I had to ask, "Who's Lily?"

"Sorry, that's what I call 'Ms. Brannon'. Ha, she'd have a good laugh being called Ms. Brannon. Most people call her Lillian but her dad and I always called her Lily. Her full name is Genevieve Lillian Brannon."

"Where are her parents? Why didn't they report her missing?"

"They died last year. Now, I'm about the only family she really has."

"No siblings?"

"No. She has an aunt but she doesn't talk to Lily anymore. Not sure why. It started after her parents died in the car crash."

"Any other family?"

"Not really. Two cousins, Charlie and Chloe. Charlie's got a drinking problem. I don't know much about Chloe. They're both a bit older than Lily and they were never close."

Annie looked down at Harry who was content with his sippy cup, now almost empty. She seemed upset about the situation with the aunt.

"I read the Missing Persons Report you sent to the Long Beach Police. Very thorough." I was surprised by the amount of information she provided about Ms. Brannon, including her drivers license and vehicle information. Most people filing a Missing Persons Report weren't able to provide accurate information or an up to date picture.

"I tried to put in everything I could possibly think of. Anything else you need to know?"

Why it took you two weeks to report her missing but I didn't think this was the time to ask.

"A few things, but I could probably use a better picture."

"Oh, I was in such a tizzy about getting all the information in I just grabbed the first photo of her I had. Probably the one of her in a fairy godmother costume at Halloween wasn't the best one to send."

"No, probably not." But, it did explain the tiara, the sparkles, the large blue gown, and the over-sized grin.

"She thought it would be funny for Harry. Her being his godmother. Harry was terrified." Harry looked up at the sound of his name and she stroked his cheek. "You sure you don't want a cup of coffee?," she asked me.

"No, some water would be nice though." I got the feeling she was going to continue to ask me if I wanted something to drink until I took something.

"Sure, so what else do you want to know?" She placed Harry down and he followed her as she got me the water.

As she handed me the glass, I asked, "Was she involved in any high risk activities?"

Annie laughed. "Sorry, if you knew her you wouldn't ask that."

It was always tough asking that question and other ones in that vein. Few wanted to admit to themselves that their friend or relative wasn't perfect; never mind admitting it to a stranger.

"No drugs? alcohol?"

"No. She never tried drugs. She got drunk once in college- with me." She looked out the window with a small smile on her face.

"Isn't is possible she started self-medicating? Drugs or alcohol could help dull the pain of the last year, the loss of her parents and aunt."

"I understand what you're asking and why you're asking but no. Sometimes she'll have a beer and I mean *a* beer. She acquired a taste for Sam Adams while she was interning in Boston." She smiled again at another memory.

"You didn't see her much though did you?"

"Every month or so. But we spoke every day, usually a couple times a day."

"When was the last time you saw her?"

"She came here for Harry's first birthday. January 11. We celebrated Lily's birthday too. Hers is the 4th."

"When was the last time you spoke to her?"

Tears welled in her eyes. "Friday night, February thirteenth at eight."

"That's very specific."

"Do you think I don't remember the last time I talked to my best friend!" She cleared her throat. "I'm sorry. We had an argument and..." and the tears welled over. I turned to look out the window while she tried to compose herself.

"I have to put Harry down for his nap. I'll be right back. Why don't you go in the living room and make yourself comfortable?"

She picked up Harry and pointed me to the next room. I could hear her going up the stairs as I walked into the living room. It was a standard living room with two couches that sat across from each other. I turned to the back wall and saw a collage of framed pictures. I went to take a closer look assuming I would see pictures of their wedding and of Harry from birth. What I saw was Lily.

She was in so many of the pictures. Lily and Annie at Annie's graduation. Lily and Annie at Annie's wedding. She must have been the maid of honor based on the other wedding photo, the one with the whole bridal party. Lily with Annie and Harry when he was born. There were other people in the photos too, Annie's husband and what I could only assume were his family. But Lily was everywhere. The outfits and the settings changed but her green eyes and smile were always there.

Annie came into the living room quietly as I was looking at the photos. "She's my best friend. A sister really. Harry's godmother. You have to find her." She spoke softly.

"Mrs. Follette, I told you I don't work in Long Beach."

"But you're a detective. You can find her." I looked back at the photos. Annie's gaze was intense and I had a feeling I wasn't going to be able to say no. I didn't think I wanted to.

I hesitated.

"Please. I'll pay you whatever I can. Jeffrey will be home shortly. He'll agree."

"It's not the money. She's been gone over two weeks. I wouldn't even know where to start."

I turned to face her and she handed me a keyring. "Start in her apartment. Here are the keys."

I took them without hesitating.

We walked over to the couches and sat across from each other.

"When was the last time you were at her apartment?," I asked her.

"Beginning of December. Jeffrey was out of town for business. Harry and I spent the week with her."

"How did she seem?"

"A little sad with the holidays coming. First one without her family. I made her put up a Christmas tree. I told her she had to do it for Harry but we both knew I thought it was best for her. But we had a good time decorating it." Annie looked back at the photos on the wall. "She's a funny girl. She can find the humor in anything. Sometimes it's only her who thinks its funny but you can't help to laugh with her." The tears started again but she tried her best to continue. "I know when you find her she'll say something funny. At least, it'll be funny to her." She smiled as she wiped the tears away.

"I have to ask again about the last time you spoke to her."

"She called me after her date. She said it didn't go well."

"She was dating someone?"

"No, it was a blind date. From a website."

"Do you think maybe her date followed her home?"

She looked at me and adamantly said, "No, no one followed her."

"You sound very sure."

"Because we always had a routine. After I graduated, Lily was living alone and that made me nervous. Maybe I was paranoid because I was pregnant, all those hormones. Jeffrey said it was because I watched too many crime shows. Anyway, I told her to take a circuitous route home, always on well populated streets, checking to make sure no one was following her. I didn't want some random guy knowing where she lived or that she lived alone."

"But you thought it was alright for her to go out with some random guy from a website?"

She didn't like that question. I got a flash of what she looked like when her husband said something she didn't like. I had seen my mother give my father that look too many times. It wasn't pretty.

"I set her up with Franklin, from the 'Journey to Love' website. He was very nice, smart, funny. I thought it was a good match."

"You set it up?"

"Yes, she was less than eager to date. She hadn't dated at all since graduating. Not one date! I thought it was time and that she just needed a little push." Her eyes blazed.

Trying to settle her down, I motioned for her to calm down. "Ok."

"Sorry, Jeffrey said I shouldn't have done it."

"What did you mean that it didn't go well?"

"No, she said he had 'crazy eyes'. Don't ask because I don't know what she meant by that." I wasn't sure what Lily had meant by crazy eyes either- did he stare too often or too intently? Was it drugs? Was it a medical condition?

Before I could ask her more about it, Annie continued. "She got really mad and hung up on me." The tears started to flow again. "She'd never done that before."

"She was home when she called?"

"Yes, getting on the elevator."

"Jeffrey said I had been too hard on her. That I should just let her calm down. We were out of town, Coudersport. There was a snowstorm and we were stuck there for a few extra days. My cell didn't have good reception there. I tried calling a few times but it always went to voicemail. I figured she lost or broke her phone, again. I thought when I got home there'd be a message on the home phone. I had a new cell phone and she probably didn't remember the new number. We got home the eighteenth but nothing. I left her messages on her home phone while we were away too. Then on Monday I called her office. First, they told me she was busy with a patient. Then she was at lunch. She never took lunch. They made her work through lunch. I kept calling and by Wednesday they said she hadn't shown up for work in over a week."

"Why didn't they tell you that the first time you called?"

"They said they thought I was a patient and they didn't want anyone to know she wasn't in. A lot of patients had stopped coming after their first visit of her not being there. So, they were calling to see if she was back. They figured I was just another one of them."

"Did they call her aunt to tell her?"

She looked at me quizzically. "I don't know but I doubt it. Why would they?"

"As her emergency contact."

"No, that would be me. And no they never called me. I'm her power of attorney too."

"Power of attorney? Why would she need one of those?" I asked. I was a bit older, six years older, and in a higher risk occupation and I didn't have one.

"Yes, I know what would a twenty three year old healthy woman need a power of attorney for? She said 'Just in case.'"

"Didn't that strike you as odd?" Not many twenty year olds even know what a power of attorney was, never mind have one. "Have you thought maybe she was planning to do something?"

"No, do not even say it. She would *not* have done that." She realized that her volume raised more than she wanted and took a deep breath. I just looked at her. "I know, I know. That's what they all say. But I know Lily, she was a planner. She saw everything that needed to be handled after her parents death and knew this would make it easier if it ever became necessary. And I think she knew Aunt

Florence wasn't going to be that person. She didn't want to admit it and I still can't but she knew. She came with the forms in September."

We both sat there in silence.

"And what about Laude?," Annie asked.

"Laude?," I asked.

"Laude, her dog. Her parents gave her Laude for graduation. She loved that dog. She would not have done anything to hurt Laude. Where is Laude?"

Good question. I had seen some dog toys at her apartment and Steve had mentioned a dog walker but I had never thought about the missing dog.

Annie continued, "Laude was always within her reach. Lily found it endearing that she followed her from room to room, even into the bathroom. I have a one year old that does that. I don't find it endearing."

A tall man walked through the front door, carrying a pizza. "Jeffrey, I'm glad you're home." Annie got up to greet him, giving him a kiss on his cheek. With Jeffrey's arm around Annie, she introduced us. "This is Detective Miccoli." I got up and we shook hands.

"Nice to meet you. You here about Lillian?"

"Yes."

"Hungry? We got plenty." Jeffrey asked.

"No, thanks. I have to go. Plans with the family."

Annie escorted me to the front door. "Wait, here a second." She ran upstairs and returned a few minutes later with a manila envelope with 'Lily' written across it. "Here, this should help. She gave this to me when she asked me to sign the power of attorney papers." I peaked inside and found keys and a printout containing account information for Lily's bills, even passwords.

I wasn't sure if Annie was foolish or just desperate to give this information to someone she had met an hour ago. "Look, I'll do what I can to find Lily."

She smiled. "I think she'd like you calling her that."

LILY

Saturday   February 28, 2009

Week one I waited for rescue.
Week two I planned escape.
Week three I tried to execute the plan.

I had thought from the start that a foot race between us would result in me losing. What I would lose was up for debate. My other plans hadn't worked. If my brilliant 'Shawshank Redemption' plan worked, it would take months. I banked on the fact that he actually liked me and wouldn't hurt Laude or me if he caught us. Making a run for it was the only option I had at the moment.

The date started like all the others. He knocked on the door, on time, and Laude and I dutifully followed him up the stairs and we sat in our respective seats.

As he went through the swinging door, I grabbed Laude and ran out the dining room door into the foyer. The chair alarm rang immediately. He would expect me to go to the left to the front door, the closest exit. I turned right and headed for the kitchen and what I hoped was an unlocked back door. I heard him screaming and the swinging door slam against the wall. I ran into the kitchen. The back door was a few feet away. His screams were closer. I refused to turn to see how close he was.

I reached for the door.

I grabbed the door knob.

It turned.
It opened.
The cold, fresh air hit me.
I felt free.
The yard lit up.
I saw the stairs too late.
I screamed as I fell down them.

Instinctively, I turned to my right trying to protect Laude. The right side of my head hit the dirt. I let Laude go. I felt his hand grab my shoulder and roll me onto my back. Laude was running around me, barking.

"What are you doing?," he asked. He didn't sound angry, just surprised.

Dazed from hitting my head, I answered "Just getting some exercise."

"Nothing like an evening run is there?"

"Nope, nothing."

I watched as he looked up at the stars and took a deep breath. I did the same. I had already known I wasn't in Long Beach. I took a deep breath and confirmed no ocean was near. Laude quieted and seemed to appreciate the fresh air too.

It was a clear night and I could see a few stars. As a child, my parents had taken me on vacation to rural Pennsylvania. The nights had been so dark you couldn't see your hand in front of your face and the stars seemed infinite. I wasn't in the country now.

I listened for anything that would tell me where I was. I faintly heard cars, a highway maybe. I could see a plane flying overhead but couldn't hear its engines. If I was on Long Island, I wasn't near either airport, LaGuardia or Kennedy.

As he assisted me up, the world swam around me. He firmly grasped my waist to steady me. I looked around in hopes of seeing neighbors startled by the screams and the barking. I was disappointed to only see trees.

With the ocean sounds finally gone I thought I would sleep better. I couldn't remember the last time I had a good night's sleep. The night after the sounds had stopped I was restless planning my escape attempt. Now, the adrenaline of the failed escape was keeping me up. Reliving what I had done, scolding myself for not running faster, for not seeing the stairs.

It was so quiet, so dark it was difficult to sleep. It seemed counterintuitive that I found it difficult to sleep because it was quiet and dark. But I was accustomed to noise. Without the television on, it was utterly silent. Eerily quiet. I was used to hearing planes overhead, people walking the streets, traffic, police and fire sirens in the distance. I had never realized how comforting those sounds were. I had wondered if Craig's noise machine had a 'city' setting. But, I knew I was in no position to ask.

Reconsidering, I knew it wasn't just the noise I missed. It was the knowing that there was someone, no, many people, out there. It was knowing that I wasn't alone.

Now, when I opened my eyes at night, there was darkness. If I turned to the right, I could see the red light of the clock radio but it didn't glow enough to illuminate the room. Even during the day I had to leave the lamp on for light. A few nights I left the television on at night, but the flickering lights were distracting. Most nights I left the bathroom light on, with the door slightly ajar, to cast a little light into the room. But that only served to remind me where I was. I was starting to feel like my elderly patients who told me how they couldn't sleep at night, how they got up several times a night to urinate and then couldn't get back to sleep. Sometimes I would find them in the lobby dozing while they waited for their appointment. I could barely keep my own eyes open in the middle of the day. I knew I needed to make some lifestyle changes. I needed to exercise. Laude's daily walks and my work shifts had been my exercise at home. I had neither here. The minimal workouts I had done my first week had stopped.

I flipped through the television stations hoping to find a workout. It took great effort to bypass the Food Network. It would only remind me of what I couldn't have. A strict diet of Rice Krispies for breakfast, a peanut butter and jelly sandwich for lunch, and soup for dinner was getting old. At least the soup selection varied. That was the biggest decision of the day- minestrone, vegetable, beef with vegetables or chicken noodle. One day I was so bored I had soup for breakfast, cereal for lunch and peanut butter and jelly for dinner.

Finally, I found a young perky woman leading a cardio workout. Normally I would have found the woman yelling at me to do ten more annoying. Today, she was helpful. She was followed by a strength class, led by a demanding woman who never stopped smiling, that I couldn't keep up with but I stuck it out. I found it sad that I couldn't do twenty pushups and that I was swearing by the fifteenth squat. A yoga class followed and again, I kept up as best I could. I looked at the clock and made a mental note to do it again tomorrow.

I was exhausted and slept better than I had in weeks, not great but better.

NATHAN

Monday March 2, 2009

Mom wasn't happy about me leaving early Monday morning. I had originally planned to stay until Wednesday but I thought I should get back to New York.

Instead of going home, I went straight to Lily's. I jingled the new keys in my pocket as I walked up to the building door. Annie had given me the four keys of Lily's she had. Each one's purpose was obvious. The big one was for the building door, the little one for her mailbox, the middle sized one a standard door key, and the last for her Toyota. I turned the building's door key in my hand, debating if this was the best thing to do. It felt weird going into someone else's home even though I had done it before. But I was never alone at crime scenes or during searches. It felt wrong to be going into someone's home without their permission and knowledge. But, I had promised Annie I would try.

"Laude, Laude, girl is that you? Are you home?" I hadn't been in the apartment ten minutes when I heard the woman's voice through the door.

I found a small, elderly woman on the other side.

"Who are you?" she asked as she tried to peer around me. "Is Laude here?" It reminded me of when in elementary school I would go to friends' houses to see if they could come out and play.

"No, sorry. I'm Nathan." I wondered how much to tell this woman about who I was and why I was here. "Lillian's friend Annie asked me to look after the place."

Disappointed, she said "Oh, so no Laude?"

"No."

"Oh, too bad. I'm June from down the hall. Where are they anyway? I haven't seen Laude in weeks. What a cutie she is!"

"Do you remember the last time you saw her?"

"I saw her most days with Susie for her afternoon walk. She's very upset about Laude. She put signs up and everything."

"I meant Lillian."

"Who's Lillian?"

"Laude's owner."

"Oh, you mean Genevieve. That's what Florence called her. I've lived in this building for forty years. Florence moved in about twenty five years ago. Genevieve was here a lot as a kid. Then, snap, one day Genevieve's here and Florence is gone." She paused and looked around. "Now that I think about it Susie mentioned something about Lillian. I didn't know who she was talking about."

"Anyway, do you remember the last time you saw Genevieve?"

"Oh, I don't know. Well, I hope she's back soon." Sadly, I knew she meant Laude.

I watched her as she continued to her apartment.

I added Susie to the list of people I needed to speak to.

To stall going through Lily's home, I called Steve on his cell phone.

After the first ring, he answered. "Hey, Nathan. What's going on? Still in Philly?"

"No, came home early. Anything new on the missing persons case?"

"No, nothing. I was just going to call her aunt. The condo's management company had her listed as next of kin. It took me a while to track her down."

Trying to save Steve some time, I told him. "She may not be much help. Annie said they hadn't had much contact recently. Annie has the power of attorney too."

"Ok."

"Why are you doing it? Shouldn't a detective be assigned?"

"Assigned to what? It's not a case."

I didn't want to argue with Steve and knew this wasn't completely his decision. He may have believed it wasn't a case but, ultimately, it was up to the chief of police.

"Wait, did you say 'Annie'? Isn't that the lady that filed the report? It doesn't say anything here about her having the power of attorney." I could hear him shuffling through more papers. "How did you know that?" I had hoped to get information from Steve without giving any about my visit with Annie. "Please tell me you didn't go see her."

Silence gave him the answer he didn't want.

"Why did you that?" We both knew why I had gone to meet Annie.

"I was so close and I was curious," I answered.

I had always been the more curious of the two of us. As kids, he'd want to play 'cops and robbers'. He was always the cop, making me the robber. I always wanted to go to the museum or the library.

Steve was destined from birth to be a police officer. His father was a police officer, his uncle and grandfather too. Maybe he didn't always know he wanted to be one, he just always knew he would be one.

I came to it later. In high school, I visited Steve and his father for a weekend. His father was a NYPD detective. Eating dinner, he told us about some of his cases. I couldn't get enough. Steve had had enough. Steve appeared content to be a patrolman and remain one until he retired.

"And that's why you're home early." It wasn't a question.

"I'll give you a call if I learn anything." I waited for Steve to say the same in return.

"You owe me a drink." He'd come around. He always did.

I sat at Lily's dining room table and wrote up my plan to find her. There was so much to do and little manpower to do it. I had two more days off of work and this was how I was going to use my time.

First on the list, meet the superintendent. At one in the afternoon, I went down to his office. The door was open and I could hear someone milling around. I knocked on the door and waited for a reply. "Yep, come in."

I walked in to find a sixty year old balding gentleman sitting at a desk, pulling on his remaining hair. He looked up, surprised to see a stranger.

"Detective Micolli, I'm looking for Ms. Brannon," I said while extending my hand.

He shook my hand, without getting up. "Oh, what a shame. Tony Vagnato. I saw the police here on Friday. One of them asked me a few questions. Any news?" He reclined in his chair.

"Not yet. I was hoping you could help me."

"How? I'm a little swamped right now. My assistant's out sick." I looked around the office and noticed everything in disarray. "Ya, I know. Franco kept everything nice and neat. I miss him. He'll be back this week."

"Sorry to hear it." I got the feeling the mess was going to get even worse with every day his assistant was gone.

"I saw a few surveillance cameras and I was hoping to see the surveillance videos."

"Sure. But, we only have the one."

"I saw a few cameras. A couple in the lobby. I figured you'd have some in the garage too."

"Two of those in the lobby are dummy cameras."

"Nothing on the floors?"

"No. Just the lobby. You can see the entrance to the elevator. That'll take me a day or two to get ready for ya. Everything's a bit of a mess."

"Yes, you mentioned that. What about the garage? Any cameras in there?"

"We did. But they broke a few years ago. Too much money to replace. I forgot about 'em."

I gave him my numbers and told him I'd be in the apartment the rest of the day if he got to it earlier.

"While I'm here, what can you tell me about Lillian?"

"Sweet girl. Her aunt moved in about the same time I started here. Lillian always tipped well. Didn't learn that from that aunt of hers. Lillian always had something wrong in that apartment or needed something done. Poor girl couldn't fix a thing. Not complaining, I'll miss that extra cash." He looked back at his pile of paperwork. I took it as my cue to leave.

I returned to Lily's apartment and stopped putting off the inevitable. I started with her answering machine. Thirteen messages. Eleven from Annie. One from Jeffrey.

"Lil, it's me. Please pick up." It was Annie. Friday night at nine.

"Lily, please. It's Annie. I'm sorry. I know you're mad. Please call me back. You have the numbers." Friday night at eleven. Each one I could hear Annie becoming more and more distraught. I would have laughed at the fifth one if Lily wasn't missing. Annie sounded just like my mother when she was mad. "Genevieve Lillian, this is juvenile! Answer the damn phone." I heard her sniffle. "I'm sorry. Please, I'm sorry. Just call me." I heard her begin to sob as she hung up.

In the middle of her many messages there was one from Jeffrey. I got the impression Annie didn't know he had called. "Lillian, if you're just mad at Annie, that's o.k. I understand." He laughed but it didn't sound genuine. He sounded upset. "Just call me so we know you're all right. Call me at work. Plus Harry wants to talk to his Auntie Lil. Please, Lillian, we're worried."

The only message not from the Follette household was from a healthcare company.

"Hi, Lillian. It's Olivia from Jupiter Healthcare. It was so good talking to you last week. I'm glad you're doing better. I left you a couple messages on your cell about some of your options for a new job. I hope you haven't changed your mind. Either way, give me a call." It was Wednesday February 18th at ten in the morning.

Annie hadn't mentioned Lily was thinking about changing jobs.

I went through the envelope Annie had given me with Lily's personal information. Annie included a note that had her own information - her email address and cell and home phone numbers. I marveled at the neatly printed sheets, in Lily's hand, containing her home address and phone number; her work address, phone number, and office manager name; her car make, model, license plate, and VIN number. Additional pages had copies of her drivers license and medical insurance card; her bank account information, including passwords; and insurance policy. The last page was the power of attorney paperwork. I was astonished and impressed by her thoroughness.

Annie hadn't added information about the date Lily had gone on. I would have to call her for that, as well as the dog walker's phone number. I had to talk to her, see if she had noticed any changes in Lily's routine or attitude. I wanted to talk to her Aunt Florence. I felt it best to wait on that until Steve had contacted her. I planned to go to Lily's office. Why hadn't they called Annie when she didn't show up for work?

NATHAN

Tuesday   March 3, 2009

I woke up early, in my rental in Queens. I had slept on the couch, again. Chinese take out boxes were still on the coffee table from the night before. I had gotten in late from Lily's and stopped by Chang's on the way home.

I often woke up to this scene after working. An arrest at the end of a shift would leave me with hours of paperwork and I'd come home with a late dinner of take out. I knew a detective position would mean more paperwork but I looked forward to the promotion. I had been working hard to get noticed, to the detriment of other areas of my life. If only I knew when I'd officially start as a detective. For now, I remained on patrol.

I got up, showered, and headed to Lily's office.

I didn't get the impression from Annie that Lily liked her job. The message regarding changing jobs confirmed it. I pulled up to the nondescript building. A few cars were out front.

The door squeaked as I entered and a young woman smiled from behind the desk. "Hello, there. How can I help you?"

"I wanted to talk to the office manager please. Rosa, I believe."

She stood up, leaned forward on the counter, placing her elbows on it; pushing her breasts together. "Well, I'm Alexa. I'm sure I can help," she purred. Did men usually respond to this act from her? Steve would have loved it.

"I'm Detective Miccoli. I'm here to talk about Lily."

"Who?" Annie had told me everyone called her Lillian.

"I'm sorry. Lillian Brannon." Alexa continued to look puzzled. I added, "Physical therapist."

"Sorry, I don't know any Lillian. We've never had a Lillian work here or at the other facilities." She sat back down and returned to her computer screen. She had lost her interest in me with my talk of another woman.

I looked around and saw the name of the company. I knew this was the right place.

Trying to spur her memory along, "She worked here until about two weeks ago."

"We had a Jen that worked here until about two weeks ago but she quit."

"What happened?" Realizing too late, I should have brought Lily's picture with me.

"Don't know. Rosa told me she didn't work here anymore"

"Ok, I need to talk to Rosa."

Completely losing interest, she pointed to the row of chairs against the wall. "Fine. She'll be here in about ten minutes. Just have a seat."

There were four empty seats, the fifth seat was occupied by an old man. I sat down next to him.

"What are you in for?" he asked. Before I could answer, "I'm here for my hip. Don't mind that one," pointing to Alexa. "Did I hear you say you're a detective?"

I cringed realizing, again, I shouldn't be introducing myself as detective. "Yes." I took a closer look at him. He looked over eighty, thin, tall, and frail.

"I'm retired NYPD, the 115."

Surprised to meet a fellow police officer here, I put my hand out. "I'm in the 109."

"Good to meet you. I'm Bernard Franks. Call me Bernie." He shook my hand heartily. There was more strength to his grip than I expected.

"Nathan Miccoli. Call me Nathan." Unlike Lily, I had no nicknames.

"What are you doing all the way out here?"

"Investigating a missing persons case."

Bernie became visibly agitated. "I knew it. You're here about Genny aren't you. I told my daughter she wouldn't have just quit. She was a responsible girl. She was the best one here."

"No, I'm sorry. I'm here about Lillian Brannon."

"Lillian? She introduced herself as Gen Brannon. I got her card here somewhere. You think we talking about the same girl? Short, thin, brown curly hair, green eyes."

He rummaged through his wallet and pulled out a business card. "Here it is," and he handed it to me. It had the facilities name, address, phone number and 'Genevieve L. Brannon, P.T.' written on it.

"Yes, that's her. Her friend who filed the report told me everyone called her Lillian."

"They all called her Genny back there. It suited her. She was a sweetie."

"You notice anything off about her in the past few weeks?"

"No, I've been coming here over a month. I started working with another therapist first. Then I switched to Genny. In the two weeks or so I worked with her she seemed fine."

"Didn't mention any personal problems?"

"No, she didn't talk about anything personal. She had me do my exercises. I'd tell her about my great grandkids. We'd laugh. She never mentioned anything personal at all now that you mention it."

Alexa called from behind the desk, "Bernard, you can go back now. James is waiting."

Bernie shook his head and raised his hand to acknowledge her.

"Now I'm back with James. That one's not nearly as nice, or as good. Genny would come up and get me. Always called me Mr.

Franks." He looked down at his watch. "She was always on time too. This one, fifteen minutes late." He struggled to get up from the chair.

I got up, offering my hand. "You need a hand?"

"No thanks." He stood straight up and grabbed his cane from against the wall. "I wish I could be more help."

"Here's my card if you think of anything else."

"I hope you find her. She's a sweetie."

He'd already said that.

Still waiting for Rosa, I stepped outside to call Annie. I needed to know anything else she had left out about Lily's work. She answered on the first ring.

"It's Nathan."

"Good news?" She sounded hopeful.

"Sorry, nothing yet. But I'm outside her work. They said they called her Genny?"

"Oh my god. That's right. I'm sorry I totally forgot! Lily was used to Aunt Florence and her mom calling her Genevieve but no one else. By the time she realized she should correct the boss about calling her Gen she thought it was too late. She resigned herself to it. Then that James started calling her Genny. He did it just to piss her off. He hated her because he thought she stole the early work shift from him."

"Anything else you want to tell me? I'm waiting for the office manager." I was looking in and could see Alexa talking to an older heavy set woman, Rosa probably. They both looked annoyed.

"James didn't like her. Sure he's thrilled she's gone."

"Why?"

"He wanted her work shifts." Not wanting to lose Rosa, I ended our conversation.

I re-entered the office and went back to the reception desk.

"Hi, Rosa. I'm Nathan Miccoli. I'm here to talk about Gen."

Looking confused, she looked from me to Alexa. "Alexa said you're here about someone named Lillian."

"Little mix-up. People here called her Gen. Anyway, when was the last time you spoke to her?"

"Couple of weeks ago."

"Can you be more precise?"

"Look, we're busy and I don't have time to talk about some girl who decided she wasn't going to show up for work anymore. I'm used to the front desk staff doing it but it's a problem when the therapist doesn't show. Damn girl couldn't even give two weeks? Just didn't show up."

"Wasn't that out of character? She was always on time. Never missed a day." Bernie had been helpful.

"I was surprised yes. But, I can't say I knew the girl. She kept to herself."

"Did you try to reach her when she didn't show?"

"Her cell phone went right to voicemail. I left her a message on her voicemail. I had better things to do than to hunt her down, like find another therapist."

"Did you call her emergency contact?"

"No, why the hell would I do that?"

"Because she's *missing*. You were the first to notice and you did nothing about it."

"Oh." She looked down. "I got to get to work." She sat down and turned to look at her mound of paperwork.

I turned from her and headed back into the treatment area. I ignored Alexa's calls from behind me of "You can't go back there."

Bernie was lying on one of the mats in the back of the gym. A chunky man, average height dressed in khakis and a yellow polo shirt sat next to him, filling out paperwork. The yellow shirt made him look jaundiced.

Bernie waved when he saw me and started to get up.

"Don't get up. I just told you you have ten more." I didn't think it was the tone you should use towards an elder, never mind a client.

"You must be James." I extended my hand to shake which he ignored. He returned to his paperwork. Ignoring James, Bernie sat up and introduced us.

"James, this is Detective Miccoli."

"I'm here about Genny. Is there somewhere we can talk privately?," I asked him.

Without looking up from his paperwork he said, "I'm busy and I have nothing to say. Didn't know the girl."

"You worked with her for seven months. You had to know something about her." I said it as nicely as I could. I had instantly disliked James when Annie had told me how he didn't like Lillian. He was confirming my opinion. My comment was met with silence.

I leaned in close, close enough that only James and Bernie would hear me. "I do know you didn't like her and that you benefitted from her disappearance." That got his attention.

James became a blubbering fool after that. Bernie tried to conceal his pleasure watching James squirm. I immediately learned James had nothing to do with Lily's disappearance. He was out of town that weekend and had ski passes, receipts, and plane tickets to prove it. He rummaged through his backpack and showed me everything and anything he could. He had left Thursday night and had proof that he'd been away over the days that Lily had gone missing.

I spoke to the ladies that worked in the billing department with Lily next. They had no information. They all said the same things about her. She was nice, quiet, good worker, patients liked her, kept to herself. They didn't notice anything different about her during her last week at work.

The trip to Lily's work yielded no results. It only made me realize how alone Lily had been.

I called Annie while driving to Lily's home. Before she could ask if I had learned anything helpful, I told her I hadn't. I needed more information from her. She seemed to be the only one that had any information about Lily.

She didn't have any information about Susie, no last name or phone number. She recommended checking her bank accounts but then remembered Lily paid her cash.

Annie balked at giving me information about Lily's date. "He had nothing to do with this. I told you that."

"I'm sure you're right. But he was the last person to talk to her."

"I was the last person to talk to her."

"Well, it appears he was the last person to see her. He could tell us how she was. What's his number?"

"I don't have it."

"You lost it?"

"No, I never had it. We communicated by the website. I never spoke to him."

It was bad enough Annie had arranged a date with a man she had never met but she hadn't spoken to him either.

"What do you know about him?"

"I can send you his picture." I assumed by the ensuing silence that was all she knew.

"Where did they meet?"

"Roaster's. Up the street from her apartment." Her sharp tone relayed her unhappiness about the question.

I knew where Roaster's was. I added the staff as more people I needed to talk to.

Harry was crying in the background and Annie wasn't happy with me. Before she could hang up, I asked, "Did Lily ever mention an Olivia from Apex Healthcare?"

Distracted by the new line of questioning, she no longer sounded annoyed. "Yeah, she had accepted a job from them out of college. It's a travel agency for healthcare workers. She opted out after her parents' accident."

"What do you mean a travel agency?"

"They find a therapist or nurse a temporary job, usually thirteen weeks, and arrange the housing. Lily was planning to take a few of those assignments around the country after college. She thought it'd be fun. Why are you asking about Olivia?"

"Because she left Lily a message on the eighteenth."

"Probably just checking in. Lily said she'd call sometimes to check on her. She hoped Lily would take a job with them."

"But she hadn't mentioned thinking about it recently?"

"No, she hadn't mentioned her in a month or so. The last time Olivia called was around the holidays. They really needed someone for an assignment. Lily said she wasn't ready."

Lily had gotten ready but never mentioned it to her best friend. What else hadn't she mentioned?

Lily's apartment building lobby was empty when I entered. I walked to the mailboxes and used the key Annie had given me and checked her mail. For not being checked in a couple weeks, there wasn't much there.

I opened the piece of mail from the city of Long Beach and learned Lily's car was in the impound. It had been towed on February 16, from the permit required lot across the street from the building, for exceeding the continuous time allowed in the parking lot.

I walked to the elevators and the one on my right opened as I got closer. I stopped, waiting for someone to get off. No one exited and

I proceeded onto the elevator, looking around for the motion detector. I stepped on and pressed five. Before the doors closed, I saw in the mirror's reflection someone entering the building. I cringed as the doors closed, knowing I should hold the elevator for them. I felt less guilty knowing they couldn't see me in the elevator.

When I entered the apartment, I headed right to the desk, where Lily had left her laptop. I had put it off yesterday but I had to look through Lily's computer. Before sitting, I opened the window and took a deep breath. I sat down and looked out onto the ocean, admiring the view. I shook my head, knowing I could sit here all day procrastinating. I took another deep breath and opened the laptop, which displayed wallpaper of Shea Stadium.

I knew this was violating Lily's privacy. I realized I had no choice and assuaged my guilt that I wasn't breaking in. Lily had provided her passwords to Annie in case of an emergency. This was an emergency.

I reminded myself that I didn't actually know Lily. She wasn't a friend or anything more. But yet that didn't seem to ring true. I repeated to myself that she was a missing person who needed my help.

I logged onto Lily's cellular phone account. The last phone call she made was to Annie. There were no additional calls made after eight Friday night. I scrolled down the call history. Most of the calls were to or from Annie. Using reverse look up, I confirmed that the calls I couldn't identify were local take out restaurants. I smiled, picturing her on the couch eating Chinese food out of the cartons after a hard days work, like I did.

I used the 'Find my iPhone' application and nothing came up. The last known location was the apartment's address.

I logged onto her bank account next. She had a checking and savings account. She had opened both in July with minimal deposits. The checking account had a small balance. She used billpay to pay most of her bills, except for the building's maintenance payments which were paid on the first with a check.

Her credit card, with the same bank, was paid off monthly. There were no charges past the twelfth. There were only a few charges since the last statement, nothing suspicious. The payment was due next week. With enough money in the checking account, I used bill pay to pay it. I made a mental note to let Annie know.

Last, I checked Lily's landline. It had a feature to check the last twenty outgoing phone calls. All were to Annie. None were made after the twelfth. The last incoming calls were all from Annie. She had called at all times of the day and night in hopes of reaching Lily.

If I had had any doubts about Lily's disappearance, they were gone. There was no way she just left of her own will. She couldn't have done that without money or a car.

I'd given Steve a day to calm down. Truthfully, I had given him a day to find out more.

I called his cell and he answered "What?" on the first ring. He hadn't calmed down as much as I had thought.

"You said I owe you a drink. Up for it tonight?"

"Sure." He was cooling down.

"Meet you at Sammie's at seven?" That would save ten minutes of back and forth deciding where to go and when to meet.

"Got it." He hung up before I could ask him anything else, which was probably for the best.

He walked into Sammie's only five minutes late, a record for him. After pleasantries, he got to why I had asked him.

"I spoke to the aunt. She wasn't any help."

"Where does she live?"

"An adult community in Hicksville."

"You go see her?"

"No, talked to her on the phone. She wasn't friendly. She didn't sound upset over her niece either."

The waitress came over and we ordered two beers.

"You learn anything new?" Even though Annie had said their relationship was strained, I hoped she might know something useful.

Exasperated, he shook his head. "What's to learn, Nathan? The girl left. The aunt doesn't care. No one cares."

"Annie cares."

"And I can see you care too and I have no idea why." Before I could answer, although I didn't have a good answer, he continued, "It's like that damn cat you found."

"I helped Roxie." In the sixth grade, we had been walking home from school on a Friday when a grey cat, with a purple collar, came up to me. Steve kept walking. I knelt down and checked the collar. It had an identification tag but it was old and I couldn't read the information. Steve yelled at me for touching a stray. 'Didn't your mom every tell you not to touch strange animals? She might have fleas, or some kind of disease. Come on, I got to get home.' He resumed walking.

I knew I couldn't leave the cat. She wasn't a stray. 'This cat has to get home too, Steve,' I pleaded.

"You became obsessed with finding that damn cat's home. Posters, ringing people's door bells."

I hadn't become obsessed. I was simply determined to find her home. Mom had helped me make posters and Dad put them up while I went house to house with Roxie and my sisters. "I found her home, didn't I?"

He took a long sip of the beer. "Yes, and for two full days that is all I heard from you. That old woman didn't even know her own name." True. The owner was an eighty year old lady with dementia who lived three blocks from where I found Roxie.

"She knew the cat's name though. And she was very thankful." I remembered the sheer joy on her face when she had opened her door to find me standing on her doorstep with Roxie. Roxie jumped out of my arms and into the house.

"Yep, she gave you *a whole dollar* to say thanks." To an elderly woman on a fixed income, that was a lot of money. Plus, she thought it was 1965.

"It wasn't the money. I didn't do it for the money. I just wanted to help."

"Yes, you and your wanting to help." He looked around, frustrated, "Where the hell is that waitress?" He found her and waved impatiently at her.

We ordered two burgers and spoke about other things until halfway through the meal. I put it off as long as I could.

"She's really missing, Steve."

"She's missing because she left and didn't tell anyone."

"Someone took her. She wouldn't just leave."

"How do you know that? You don't know her. You think you know her so damn well because you spent some time with her friend? A friend who took two weeks to report her missing." He then mumbled "some friend" before taking another sip of beer.

"There were reasons for that. But, Lily wouldn't just leave."

"Who?"

"People call her Lillian. Annie calls her Lily."

"You realize you sound ridiculous. You're looking for someone you don't even know. And, I'm telling you, there is no evidence saying she was taken."

"Come on. How did she leave? Her car was in the impound."

"She took a train or a bus or a plane." He took a drink and looked around the restaurant. He stopped and turned back to me, eyes focused. "And how the hell do you know her car is in the impound?"

"I checked her mailbox."

"Nathan, you know you cannot go through someone's mail!"

Ignoring him, I continued. "And why would she leave and not take anything but Laude?"

"What the hell is a 'Laude'?"

"The dog. Steve, her closet and dresser drawers are full of clothes. Her suitcase is there. Her computer is there." I paused then added, "And what money did she use? She didn't use her ATM or credit cards."

We stared at each other in silence. The silence ended when he realized I knew too much.

"How do you know she didn't take anything? How did you notice all of that? You were only in her apartment a few minutes."

I wanted to say because I was a good detective but a comment like that would not help me get Steve's help. It would only infuriate him. I took a sip of beer and he pieced it together.

The lightbulb went off, "You have been in her house legally, right?"

"Now who's being ridiculous. Of course it's legal. Annie gave me the keys." I was insulted he even had to ask.

"Please tell me Annie told you about the credit cards, too. You can't run her financials from work! You know they monitor everything. You're still in a probationary period aren't you?"

"Annie gave me the information. And no, I'm not on probation. I haven't even started as a detective yet. I know I have no jurisdiction in the case. But you have to agree there is a case."

We finished our meals and our beers. The waitress brought us another round.

"If, and I do mean, *if* she was taken. Who took her?"

"I don't know."

"Do you have any leads?"

"No."

"Any ideas?"

"I was going to check out the video surveillance in the building. See if I could firm down when she went missing. Check her bank accounts more closely."

"And how are you going to do all of that? You don't have jurisdiction."

"But I do have passwords and usernames." If I had had any doubts that Lily had left unwillingly, they were squelched. Someone took Lily and I was going to find her and bring her home.

Steve got up and finished his beer. "I just hope this lasts only two days." I didn't say it to Steve but that was wishful thinking. I had a bad feeling it would take me more than two days to find her, especially since I had started four days ago.

NATHAN

Wednesday   March 4, 2009

I got up early for round two with Tony. I stopped at Roasters before going to the apartment building and ordered two cups of coffee. The morning staff didn't recognize Lily's or Franklin's picture and none had been working that Friday night.

Annie had emailed me Franklin's picture and email address last night. She responded to my email regarding more information on him curtly. She hadn't heard from Franklin since the date. His profile on the 'Journey to Love' website was no longer posted. She couldn't remember anything specific about him. I sent an email to him but had not received anything back yet.

After I entered Lily's building, I stopped. I stood in the lobby and tried to see it like Lily would. If she entered through the front door, the two elevators where fifteen feet away. The lobby was relatively narrow. A mirror hung on the left wall; I guessed to make the area feel bigger. When she entered through the front door, she would only be able to see the elevators. She wouldn't be able to see Tony's office, which was off to the right; the mailboxes, which were to the left; or the two exits to the garage and staircases, which were around the corner from each elevator.

Someone could have waited for her on either side and taken her by surprise. I hoped the video cameras provided views of the three entries.

I was sitting in the lobby when Tony got off the elevator and unlocked his office. I gave him a couple minutes to settle in before disturbing him.

"Hi again, Tony. Got you some coffee." As Steve had pointed out, I had no jurisdiction. If Tony told me to leave, I had no recourse.

Tony was sitting at his desk and looked up. "Thanks," he said as he accepted the coffee. "Sorry about the other day. I'm a little stressed with Franco out sick." I sat down in the chair against the wall as he took a sip. He looked at the cup. "This is good. I don't think I've ever had Roasters' coffee. Franco went there most days. He always offered to get me some. I always declined." He looked around the mess of his office. "Don't know what I'm going to do if he doesn't get better soon. The flu is brutal this year."

We sat and drank our coffees. I didn't want to push on the videos right away. I bought myself some time. I pulled out the picture of Franklin. "You recognize this guy?"

Tony pulled his glasses out of his pocket. He looked at it intently. Handing the picture back, he said, "No, sorry. You think he has something to do with Lillian?"

"No, but it was worth a shot."

We finished our coffee in silence. I surveyed the office and felt bad for the sick assistant. The office would only get worse with every day he missed.

"I'll get those videotapes for you. I don't think Lillian has a VCR. At least I didn't set one up for her. She might have one in a closet or something. You'll probably have to watch them here." Tony walked over to a television with a VCR in the corner. "I keep this to watch the playoffs. Here's all the tapes. I only keep them for a month. Each tape holds a day's activities. The one marked 'one' is the first of the month, two for the second, and so on. I don't think I've ever watched them. It's a quiet building." He turned on the television and looked back to me. "Hope it helps."

When Tony explained the surveillance system, I knew the tapes would be useless. The poor resolution and bad camera angle confirmed it. The angle of the camera showed only the elevators to the lobby. The two other entrances were not visible. Images were displayed every five seconds. I sighed knowing my morning would be wasted watching the tapes. I looked around and realized Tony had left.

I put in the tape labeled "13". The timer read eight in the morning. I watched as people came and went. Images showed someone getting off the elevator, then in the lobby, the next out of the building and out of sight. I started to fast forward but stopped when I saw a woman with a small black dog. From the pictures I had found in Lily's apartment, I figured it was Laude. The tall woman walking her must be Susie, the dog walker. I confirmed it when I saw Lily with the dog at six twenty in the evening. I had seen Lily come home from work at five. She had changed since coming home into the outfit Annie had described. Lily and Laude came back ten minutes later. Lily left at six forty five for the date Annie had arranged. She appeared again at eight, at the building's door, on her cellphone. The next shot had her a step away from the elevator, cell phone no longer at her ear. She never appeared on the tapes again.

I watched the fourteenth, fifteenth, sixteenth, and seventeenth. I fast forwarded through them and didn't see Laude or Lily.

Tony came back into the office, "You find anything?"

"No. Last time she was on the tape was on Friday the thirteenth. I'm going to watch a few days before the thirteenth. That ok?"

"Sure. I have things to do on the floors so I won't be in here."

"And, you said there are no other cameras?"

"No, sorry. Never seemed necessary. The building's board thought the lobby was the only entrance that needed them."

"Did Lillian usually use the front entrance?"

"As far as I know. I didn't see her too much. But I'd see her once in a while before I finished my shift. She'd either be coming in from work or walking Laude. She came and went by the front door then."

"Thanks."

I went back to February the ninth and watched the full week of tape. Lily had a routine; not good if she did have a stalker. She took Laude out shortly after six in the morning, went to work at seven. The dog walker took Laude out at noon. Lily returned at five in the evening. She took Laude out again at six and somewhere between nine and ten in the evening.

I watched Lily's neighbors come and go. I occasionally saw Tony, always in his navy uniform. I saw a few people stop to talk to Laude. Lily would smile. The camera angle gave no access to the street. After thanking Tony again for his time and use of his office, I went outside and walked around the perimeter of the building. There were no businesses in the area. It was strictly residential. The surrounding residences did not have any surveillance cameras. The stop light at the corner did not have a red light camera. There was no way for me to find if anyone followed her regularly.

The tapes were of no help other than to confirm the last time Lily was seen was at eight Friday night.

Weeks later, I would reprimand myself for not noticing what was not there.

As I re-entered the building, the tall woman who I thought was the one walking Laude was coming out. I held the door open for her and asked "Susie?" as she passed me. The resolution was poor on the video and I could be wrong.

She had been looking at the dog who was sniffing my shoes and looked up surprised, "Yes."

"Hi, I'm a friend of Lillian's. I was wondering if I could ask you a few questions."

"I'm sorry. I don't know a Lillian." She looked down at the black poodle and said "Come on, Penny." They started to walk away.

I followed her, "Wait. I wanted to talk to you about Laude."

She stopped and turned to look at me. Smiling, she said "Oh, Laude. I miss that little scamp."

I reminded her, "Lillian is her owner."

"Of course. Sorry. I don't see the owners much." Penny was pulling her towards the corner. "Sorry, Penny's really gotta go."

I knew the only way I could speak with Susie was if I went with her. "I can walk with you."

"Alright." As we stopped at the corner, waiting for the light to change, she asked, "Do you know where Laude is? I can't believe Lillian would just take her away without telling me."

"I'm looking for both of them. I don't think she'd take her away without telling you either. She knew how fond of Laude you are."

Susie nodded. "I miss Laude."

"I saw those posters you put up for Laude." She had placed several in the neighborhood. There was a large picture of Laude, under "LOST DOG." The picture of Laude was much better than the one Annie had provided of Lillian for the Missing Persons Report. I had written down the number planning to call her later today to discuss Lillian. "Did anyone call you with any tips about Laude?"

The light changed and we crossed the street. "No. Not one. Maybe I should have put up a reward. That probably would have gotten a few calls. Probably just cranks, though."

"Probably," I agreed. "When was the last time you saw Lillian?"

"The day she hired me. I'm in the building during the workday. I don't see most of the owners."

"When was the last time you talked to Lillian?"

"The day she hired me."

I couldn't believe she hadn't talked to Lillian in months. "You've been working for her for seven months and you never talked to her?"

"No. No need. I'd leave her notes daily so she knew I was there. She'd leave me cash on Fridays for the week's walks. She'd leave me a note if she had a day off but that was about it. Laude is such a good dog. I never had to talk to Lillian."

We stopped while Penny sniffed at a patch of grass. "Did you notice anything different about the apartment in the last few weeks?"

Susie turned to face me. She didn't look pleased about the question. "No. I barely leave the entryway of her apartment. I come in. Laude runs up to me. I go in the closet and take out her leash. We go out. The farthest I go into her place is the kitchen counter to leave the note."

I was slowly realizing that Susie was not going to be helpful about anything but Laude.

"Notice anything different about Laude?," I asked.

The mention of Laude put Susie in a better mood. Smiling, she answered, "Nope. She's such a good little pup. Everyone loved Laude." I had run out of questions and had learned nothing helpful.

"I appreciate your time." I handed her my card. "If you think of anything else, please give me a call." Realizing I never mentioned I was a police officer, I hoped she wouldn't ask me why the NYPD was looking for Lillian. She put the card in her pocket and kept walking Penny. I added, "Or if anyone calls with information on Laude."

"Sure." I could have walked with Susie and Penny further but it was pointless. I watched as they continued their walk. I turned around and returned to the apartment.

I went upstairs to Lily's apartment. I had to work tomorrow but thought I had enough time to go through her apartment. I had taken a cursory look on Monday but needed to take a closer look at everything. It was neat, but not compulsively so. Her kitchen had the basics- standard refrigerator, dishwasher and oven. A microwave was on the counter. The cabinets also held the basics, nothing special. The garbage was half full and I took it out to the incinerator down the hall.

Mrs. Roberto was stepping off the elevator. "Hi, Nathan. How are you?"

"Fine. Thank you. And you?" She was wearing a bright pink outfit and was holding a winter jacket in her hand.

"Heard you talked to Susie. Thought you were just watching the place for Genevieve."

"Just curious where they went."

"Tony says you're police."

This woman did keep a close eye on the building. If anything had been out of place, she would have noticed.

"I've never seen a police officer take such an interest." She looked down to the garbage bag I was holding. "Never saw one take the trash out either. And my sister was married to a cop for twenty years. Cheating bastard."

"Um, well. Just trying to help. I don't want her to come back to a smelly kitchen."

"Neighbors appreciate that too. Thank you. We don't need any bugs."

"You're welcome." She started walking towards her apartment. "Have you seen anything out of the ordinary lately?"

She turned around, giving me a piercing glare. "What do you mean?"

"Anyone hanging around the building you don't know."

"No. Winter's pretty quiet. We get plenty hanging around in the summer though."

"You see anyone visiting Genevieve that you didn't recognize? Anyone new?"

"No. No one visits Genevieve. Just Tony and Franco. One of them was always going in there."

"Yeah, Tony mentioned that."

"Poor girl couldn't fix a thing. She could use a man like you around the house." She looked me up and down, far more closely than I thought an eighty year old woman would. "She wouldn't have to pay you like she does Tony. Although you'd want some other form of payment I'm sure. They all do." She smiled and went to her apartment. I was glad she couldn't see me trying to suppress a laugh. I liked Mrs. Roberto. I might not like having her as a neighbor but she shot it straight.

Returning to the apartment, I flipped through Susie's notebook that was at the edge of the counter. It was mostly filled with Susie's accounts of Laude's walks. Notes detailed who Laude met, how good she was, and what she did on their walks. Lily would comment sometimes but usually on a Friday she just wrote "Thank you."

I looked through the hallway closet. A mixture of jackets, from heavy to light, hung from the rod and scarves, hats and gloves were organized by color on the shelf above them. Storage containers were on the right side of the closet, labeled. I peaked in the top one, labeled 'Christmas' and found Christmas decorations. Laude's leash, that Susie had said hung in the closet, was not there.

The bathroom was next. It was small but functional. The medicine cabinet had hair gels, hair spray, and mouth hygiene items. There were no medications. The under sink storage had her blow dryer and a small make up bag. Either of my sisters easily had double the amount of hair products and cosmetics.

Like every other room, the bedroom was neat. I looked through the dresser drawers and closets and found what every woman had- clothes, clothes, and more clothes. And shoes, lots of shoes. I had hoped to find a journal that would give me more insight into Lily. I was disappointed but not surprised.

There was a light layer of dust throughout. I noticed a void in the dust, oval shaped, about eight inches across. Nothing else appeared missing. There was also nothing personal anywhere. No photos, no knick knacks in any of the rooms. The whole apartment was impersonal. I realized my home wasn't much different. Pictures from my sisters' weddings were shoved in drawers, despite Mom putting them in frames.

I pulled my cell phone out. I thought a screaming child had answered the phone until I heared Annie yelling hello. It was like when I called my sister, Danielle.

"It's Nathan," I told her.

"I know that," she sounded exasperated.

I hesitated waiting for Harry to stop crying but proceeded when I realized that wasn't going to happen. "What did Lily have on her bedroom dresser?"

"What?"

"I think there's something missing from her dresser. I was wondering what it was."

Sounding even more exasperated, she answered, "I have no idea Nathan. I don't have a photographic memory of her apartment!"

I hung up, realizing it was a ridiculous thing to call about. How could a small missing object help me?

I retreated out of the bedroom. I had felt uneasy being in there. I went through the open dining living room area and out the door onto the patio. The air was cool but calm. I took a deep breath of the ocean air, while standing against the rail. I asked myself why I hadn't moved to Long Beach instead of Queens after the academy. Probably because living this close to Steve wouldn't be good for either of us. We would feel compelled to go out weekly which would force us to realize we really didn't have much in common. We shared a past. We both worked as police officers but that was where the similarities ended.

Plus, the commute would have been rough. As I watched the sun go down, the waves crashing on the shore, I wondered if it would be worth it. I sat on the lounge and wondered what it would be like to be here with Lily.

I reviewed what I had learned so far. Susie knew nothing. According to Steve, Aunt Florence didn't know anything and didn't care. The building's surveillance videos showed little. It seemed like Lily disappeared at eight o'clock Friday night. She got on that elevator and was never seen again.

I woke up on the couch, again. But this time it was Lily's. I looked around to see what had woke me.

"Annie?," I answered the ringing phone.

She was yelling about something, going too fast for me to catch on.

"Annie, slow down. I have no idea what you're talking about."

"It was a Precious Moment figurine. Her father gave it to her. It had a small chip on it. I hit it by accident with my bag in college. She was so upset!"

I sat in silence as she rambled on about the incident, about the figurine's details and about how she was too frazzled to think clearly when I called earlier.

"She was very protective about it after that."

We hung up and stared at the phone. I wasn't sure if it was helpful that I knew what the missing object was. It was too late to go home so I set an alarm on my cell phone for six in the morning and went back to sleep.

NATHAN

Thursday   March 5, 2009

While my partner went to get us lunch, I called Steve. He was glad to hear from me until I brought up Lily. I guess he had thought I had lost interest in the case. He gave me Florence's address and started to hang up.

"Wait," I urged him.

"What?"

"There's something missing in Lily's apartment."

"What?," he repeated.

"A Precious Moment."

"A what?" He was more agitated with each question.

I started to recite how Annie explained it but knew that's not what he wanted to hear. "A figurine. Her father gave it to her. It was very special to her."

"Then she obviously took it *when she left*."

"She didn't leave Steve. I'm telling you someone took her."

"Fine. Do you want me to do? I don't think her home was burgled for a figurine. Should I file a write up a Missing Figurine Report?"

He hung up before I could respond.

NATHAN

Friday   March 6, 2009

After showering, I went into the bedroom to get dressed. The small spot without dust nagged at me.

Whoever took Lily and Laude, they had to have access to the building. They had to have taken them from the apartment, avoiding the lobby and its cameras. It would have to be a strong man to carry Lily and Laude down five flights of stairs, especially if she was struggling.

But why take the figurine?

I took the garbage down to the compactor room and stared at the shoot's opening, after dropping the trash in. Lily and Laude were small enough to fit through it. The figurine could have been a souvenir.

I called Steve.

"So, now you think she's dead?"

"No, no. She's not dead. Can't be dead. Tony would have noticed that in the trash." I tried to shake the vision of what he would find if the compactor had been used on their bodies. Assuming he only ran the compactor on weekdays, the decomposing stench when he went into the room that Monday would have been strong.

"I'm wondering who in the building has a criminal record. Who could have overpowered her in her hallway and then carried her out? A workman or delivery person would have stood out that late on a Friday night. It has to be someone in the building."

"Even if that's true, do you really think that person would keep her alive for weeks? This is ridiculous, Nathan. We have to find you a girl."

He didn't understand. That was what I trying to do.

I was happy and surprised that Steve had called back. There was one person in the building with a criminal record- Gregory Straub, apartment 6P.

He had a restraining order against him and an arrest and conviction for breaking that restraining order.

After my shift, I rushed to see Tony, to learn what he knew about him. I stopped at Roaster's and grabbed two coffees, hoping that would loosen Tony's tongue. While waiting, I asked the workers if they were working Friday the 13th. The two of them had been working that night but neither recognized Lily's and Franklin's pictures.

I ran into the building, hoping Tony was still working and was glad to find him at his desk.

"Tony, good to see you. Working late?"

"Just trying to finish up. What can I do for you?"

"Wondering what you know about Gregory Straub in 6P?"

He took a deep breath and sighed. "It's his mother's condo. But I saw him a lot around here earlier in the year. I was afraid he'd moved in. The board needs to approve that. I don't want to get involved. Why you asking? You got a problem with him?"

"No, just curious."

"You know. Now that you've mentioned it. I haven't seen him lately."

"You ever see him with Lillian?"

He contemplated that for a minute. "No. Never saw her with anyone except Laude since she moved in."

I knocked on 6P's door. Mrs. Straub answered the door quickly.

"Hi, I'm Nathan. I'm helping out a friend in the building." I pulled out Lily's picture. "Do you know this girl?"

"Sure, that's Genevieve. She lives on the fifth floor. My son told me she has a real cute dog."

She gestured for me to come in. "Something wrong with her?," she asked as we sat at the dining room table. Mrs. Straub had a corner unit, a bigger apartment than Lily's, including another bedroom.

"Hopefully nothing. Did you know Genevieve well?"

"I know she'd visit her aunt a lot and then she moved in. Florence died right? That's what Tony said."

I didn't correct her. "Why'd Tony tell you that?"

"I had mentioned to him I hadn't seen Florence. He said he thought she died."

"Were you close to Florence?"

"Oh no," she answered quickly. She hesitated. "You know Florence?"

"No, ma'am," I planned to go see her on my next day off.

"She was...." She searched for the right word. "unpleasant."

"Really?" I was surprised. Annie had not given me that impression.

"Only if Genevieve was around was she pleasant. Without her, permanent frown on her face. Would barely say hello. I was afraid Genevieve was like that too. I ran into her in the elevator once but she was sweet. Just sad. Then Tony told me about Florence so I figured she was upset about. I assumed Florence was an old maid, no children and all. Just Genevieve."

Again, I didn't correct her about Florence.

"Does your son know Genevieve?"

"I know he's run into her. He's real fond of her dog. I'm sorry. Do you want something to drink?," she asked as she got up.

"No thanks." I followed her into the kitchen. The kitchen window looked out onto the ocean. I watched the calm waves as they lapped on the shore, as Mrs. Straub poured two glasses of water.

"Gregory's had a rough time lately. The wife being gone and all. He really perked up after meeting that dog. I started to tell him he should ask Genevieve out but he's a bit older than her. And a mother shouldn't meddle, right?"

I smiled in agreement.

"He's been real happy lately. He hasn't been here as much. I think he may be dating."

LILY

Friday   March 6, 2009

It was almost a week before I was let out of the room again. I assumed I was being punished for my escape attempt. As the days wore on, I missed a good meal. In a weird way, I missed Craig.

Craig still walked Laude three times a day. He never spoke to me. We had plenty of food. The pantry was restocked with the same food- cereal, bread, cans of soup. I had clean clothes.

Wednesday he "called" and asked me out for Friday. "Just casual" he had said. I wasn't sure what that meant.

When he opened the door, we stood in awkward silence. I wasn't sure who was more mad or who thought they were owed an apology more. This was feeling more and more like we were dating.

He was casually dressed in jeans and a blue T-shirt. His blues eyes were even bluer than usual. His jaw was set, his expression neutral. He shrugged and turned to ascend the stairs.

The silence continued as Laude and I followed him up the stairs and into the kitchen. This was probably what he meant by 'casual'; dinner in the kitchen. I guess he figured since I'd seen it when I ran through it last week, we could have dinner in here. I hadn't noticed anything about it then. It was a blur when I had run through it and my head was swimming when he had helped me back in.

Probably, he just didn't want me out of his sight. Laude's bed was next to the barstool at the kitchen's island he directed me to. We were eating at the kitchen's island tonight. I sat down and watched him go to the refrigerator and pull out two Coca-Colas. I felt my mouth water. I hadn't had a soda in weeks. He twisted the cap and I heard the fizzing of the carbonation escaping. He poured each bottle into a tall clear glass and brought them over to the island.

Before I could help myself I said, "Thank you."

I closed my eyes and took a deep inhale. The bubbles tickled my noise. I took a big sip and then put the glass down and exhaled "Ahh". I opened my eyes to find Craig grinning, holding his glass out, waiting for me to toast.

I tried my best to look apologetic. "Sorry. I was really thirsty."

He laughed, raising his eyebrows, "Obviously. I have plenty if you want more."

"Great." I picked up my glass, clinked his glass, and took another sip. I savored the flavor of a drink other than water. After taking a sip himself, he placed the drink on the other side of the island and directed his attention to the oven. I couldn't see what lay inside but it smelled delicious. Then the smell hit me. I took a deep inhale and said, "Oh my god. Is that pizza?"

"Yes. Thought you'd like it." He turned and gave me a prize-worthy smile. For not the first time, I thought about how handsome he was. He turned his attention to the fixings for a salad. He was wearing worn jeans, that fit just right; not loose that they were hanging off of him like the teenagers wore; not obscenely tight that it left nothing, and I do mean nothing, to the imagination. I told myself I was looking for a cell phone in his back pockets but I was admiring his behind. Additionally, there was no phone.

I shook my head to bring myself back to the present. With his back still turned, I looked around for a phone, a landline. There wasn't one. I wasn't surprised. I wouldn't have had one if Aunt Florence hadn't already had one in the condo. It was easier to keep it then to cancel the service. All I really needed was my cell phone. Craig was probably the same.

He used a pizza board to get the pizza out of the oven. The aroma was intoxicating. The cheese was bubbling. Laude started getting excited and began barking. It was one of the few 'people food' items I gave her. I would tear off a small piece of crust and she'd jump up to snatch it out of my hand. She would always start running and barking when I came home with it. I didn't know if she recognized the word pizza or the smell.

Craig looked down at Laude, who was running around the island barking. "I've never seen her so animated at dinner time."

"She likes pizza, too."

"She does?" He looked at me quizzically. He then looked down at her as she circled his legs and asked her "Do you get a slice, too?"

Answering for her, "No, just a little piece of the crust."

"Sure." He pulled off a piece of the crust and blew on it to cool it. He held it out to her and she took it from him and ran to her bed.

"You're more generous with her than I am. I usually give her a little piece."

"We have plenty."

He cut the pizza into eight slices. I thought I could eat four slices easily. I smiled at the thought that if this was a real relationship I would probably take one slice and then feign being full. This was definitely not a real relationship. I didn't know what it was.

The crust was irregularly shaped. "Did you make this?," I asked.

"Yes, my mom taught me. She was from Italy."

"Really?"

"Yes, really. What are you more surprised by, that I can cook or that I'm Italian?"

I wasn't sure. His brown hair and blue eyes didn't make me think he was of Italian descent.

I dodged answering by taking a bite. It was heavenly. It was perfect. The crust was thin and delicious. The sauce had a little kick, and wasn't sweet. It had the perfect amount and blend of cheeses.

"She was from northern Italy. There are plenty of blue eyed, blonds from Italy."

I looked up from my pizza and looked at his hair. It wasn't blond; it was brown. As I looked at it closer, I realized it was a lighter brown than a few weeks ago.

"Oh, I forgot. I colored it. In a few weeks it'll be back to normal, blond. I was surprised you didn't mention it on our first date. It was pretty dark in my profile photo." I flashbacked to what Annie had said about him - his black hair contrasted with his blue eyes. My heart sank that even if she put it together that it was Franklin who had kidnapped me she wouldn't have an accurate description. He barely looked like Franklin from our first date; who knows what his online photo was. Dyeing his hair was another way to conceal his identity. It was another sign of how much thought and planning he had put into the kidnapping.

The concern didn't slow my appetite. I took another bite of pizza and finished my soda.

He got up and got me another soda. I finished my slice, except for a small piece of crust that I gave to Laude, who was sitting by my side. She had stared at me while I had eaten the slice. After finishing her piece, she ran over to Craig and sat at his feet in hopes of another piece. She thought it was good, too.

"It's delicious. Can I have another slice?," I asked.

Craig smiled. "Sure. Take as much as you want. I'm glad you like it."

We ate without further conversation. Two sodas and two slices filled my stomach. I couldn't remember the last time anything had tasted that good or when I had eaten so much.

I watched him finish his slice. I smiled as he gave Laude a piece of his crust. I thought the bubbles had gone to my head. It felt like a real date. It was a date I enjoyed. I was uncomfortable at my attraction to him. I wondered if he could tell.

As was the plan from the moment I had sat down, I offered to help him clean up. He gladly accepted the help and when he wasn't looking I wrapped a knife with a napkin and slipped it into my pants. I had been distracted by my attraction to him for most of the meal but it didn't distract me from my latest escape strategy.

NATHAN

March 6, 2009

After finishing my water, I politely exited. Mrs. Straub's talk of Gregory's mysterious behavior, spending a lot of time on his computer, and her belief he may be dating, reminded me of Franklin.

I heard a scuffle and a cry when the phone answered. "Annie? It's Nathan."

Harry was crying harder now as she answered. "Sorry, Nathan. Harry had the phone."

"Have you heard from Franklin?," I asked.

"No. Why would I? It's been weeks since their date."

"He didn't respond to my email."

"I told you his profile was gone when you first asked for the information on him. He wouldn't have access to the email anymore."

"Don't you think that's strange?," I asked. "Franklin goes on one date with Lily and is no longer on the dating site."

"No. Maybe his membership ran out. Maybe he went on a successful date and doesn't need 'Journey to Love' anymore. He was *really* handsome." She contemplated that for a moment and then continued. That explained why she still had his photo, but nothing else. "Maybe he cancelled it after the date with Lily. She probably turned him against internet dating. Lily was really unhappy about the whole thing- before and after. So, I doubt she was happy during the date."

They were all plausible reasons. I'd gone out with my fair share and had never called them again. If he did get the email, why would he respond? I doubted I would respond to an email from someone saying they were a police officer, wanting information on a date.

"Why'd you pick him?," I asked. I wanted to know the type of man she saw Lily with. For investigative purposes only, I tried to tell myself.

She hesitated. "I don't know. Thought she had to start with somebody."

"What do you mean?"

"Nathan, he has nothing to do with this. She was home when I talked to her. She was safe in that building. Did you see the video tape? Did you see anything on it?"

"Yes, I watched the videos. It's pretty low budget stuff. I could barely make out anyone on it."

"But you saw her? After I spoke to her, you saw her, right?"

"I saw her get on the elevator that Friday night but she never appeared on the video again."

"Are you sure?," she asked.

"Yes, I'm sure."

"But she had to take Laude out that night. She had to take Laude out in the morning," she started to ramble. "She couldn't have just disappeared!," she cried.

But somehow Lily had.

LILY

Monday   *March 9, 2009*

I got to work with the knife once I heard Craig's car leave. It had taken great willpower not to try it over the weekend. I tried to cut through the wood over the window first, unsuccessfully. Pulling the nails out would be the only way to get the wood off the wall. I continued to picture a small basement window on the other side.

It was tedious work. To make the time go faster, I daydreamed of escaping through it. I'd pull over the dresser; open or break the window; place Laude through it and then pull myself through.

It was getting late and Craig would be home soon. Only half the nails were out. I tried to pull the wood away from the remaining nails but it was firmly in place. Resigned to spending another night here, I hid the nails I had removed in one of the drawers. I stepped away and looked at my work. Only if you got close to the picture could you see the missing nails.

I slept fitfully. I truly believed I would escape tomorrow. I knew I'd need a good night's sleep. Counting nails coming out of wood didn't help.

NATHAN

Monday   March 9, 2009

My next day off I visited 'Aunt Florence'. I called Steve who was glad to hear from me until I brought up Lily. I guess he had thought I had lost interest in the case. He gave me Florence's address and hung up.

I drove out to her new home, in the adult community. It was a large apartment building with a brick fascade. I flashed my badge at the security guard, who raised the gate without asking any questions. If only getting Florence to talk had been so easy.

When I entered the lobby, the overweight, bespectacled lady at the desk greeted me. I flashed my badge again and said I was here to see Florence McGowan. She directed me to her room on the second floor.

As I walked down the hallway, I noticed most of the doors were decorated for St. Patrick's Day. But, not Florence's. Her name, under the door bell, was the only distinction between her door and unoccupied rooms.

I knocked. "Who is it?" I could hear her footsteps getting closer to the door. She didn't sound pleased to have an early day visitor.

"It's Nathan Miccoli. I'm here about your niece."

There was a pause. I didn't hear her coming any closer to the door.

"What is this about?"

"Your niece, Lillian." I remembered belatedly that Lily's aunt and mother called her Genevieve. "I mean, Genevieve."

"Who let you in?" I guess she didn't want to reminisce. This was harder than I thought. Steve had told me she wasn't friendly on the phone but I expected her to open the door.

"I'm from NYPD."

She opened the door but stood in the doorway. She was obviously not inviting me in.

"I talked to the other police officer on the phone." A scowl was firmly on her face. This could not have been the same woman that Annie referred to as a loving aunt.

The deep wrinkles across her forehead led me to believe the scowl was often on her face, just as Mrs. Straub had said. Her brown hair was streaked with grey. Her glare at me, through squinting eyes, only brought more attention to the wrinkles around her eyes.

"I know, Mrs. McGowan. Officer Whitby told me. I have a few follow up questions. May I come in?" In another time and place, I would have laughed at calling Steve 'Officer Whitby'.

An old couple walked by and tried not to stare. They did not succeed. I smiled at them. Florence didn't even look at them. When they were halfway down the hall, she said, "I have nothing to say. I don't know where she is. I haven't spoke to her in months."

"Maybe you could tell me about her. Maybe you could tell me something that would help me find her."

She was aggravated when she opened the door. Now, she was furious. "*I told you* I do not know anything. I do not want anything to do with this. You have no jurisdiction anyway." She started to close the door.

"A Missing Persons Report can be filed where a person was last seen." It was a true statement but not the truth in this situation.

"I told you to leave," and she slammed the door in my face. I stood there shocked. How could she not care that Lily was missing?

I debated knocking and trying again. Instead, I turned to find three old ladies watching me. I didn't know how long they had been there.

"Have a nice day, ladies," I said as I was walked by them.

They smiled and one said "You, too, young man."

By the time I got to the lobby, the front desk woman was on the phone. I could hear Florence's voice reprimanding the woman for letting me in. She glared at me as I walked by. I drove to the guard shack and the guard waved to me as he let the gate up. I heard the phone ring and called out to him, "Might want to let that ring, buddy."

He looked perplexed but answered the phone. I looked in the mirror, saw him holding the phone away from his ear and knew I was right.

I had the rest of the day free so I headed back to Lily's. I smiled when I saw several parking spots available in front of the apartment building. In the summer when I came here for a day at the beach, I would circle for twenty minutes looking for a parking spot.

After parking, I headed to the boardwalk. It was a beautiful day, sunny and warm, about sixty degrees. I sat on one of the benches and watched the waves crash. I thought about Aunt Florence. Annie had said she had been a doting aunt and that she was like a second mom to Lily. Annie had been shocked how over the past months she had distanced herself from Lily. I closed my eyes and tilted my head up to the sky to enjoy the warmth of the sun. After a deep breath, I felt someone sit next to me. I opened my eyes and saw Mrs. Roberto to my right.

"How are you, Nathan?" She smiled and then looked at the ocean. Her outfit today was as bright as the sun. It was as yellow as the sun, too.

"Fine. You, Mrs. Roberto?"

"Great. You can call me June. Genevieve called me Ms. June." She maintained her gaze straight ahead on the ocean.

"Ok, Ms. June. Enjoying the warm day?"

"I enjoy the boardwalk every day. Why aren't you working?"

"Day off." I had worked the previous four days, even picking up an extra shift. I'd be back at work tomorrow. One of the negatives of my job was an inconsistent schedule. "I saw Florence today."

"How is she?"

"Don't know. She wasn't exactly welcoming."

"Oh. She must be pretty upset about Genevieve. To lose her sister and then Genevieve, that's pretty tough."

"I didn't get that impression."

"You must be wrong. She doted on that child."

"That's what Lily's, I mean Genevieve's, friend said too. I thought maybe she exaggerated." I had started to doubt Annie's impression of the relationship.

"No. Genevieve was here a lot growing up. Spent most of the summers here. I told you I lived here a long time. Longest resident of The Presidents Terrace." She smiled proudly.

"Even in college Genevieve spent the summers here too. Would bring her roommate...Annie."

This woman had some memory. I wondered if she kept a book by her door marking everyone's comings and goings. It wouldn't be the first one I'd ever seen. People like that could be helpful or annoying. Thankfully, Ms. June seemed to be the former.

"Annie told me she enjoyed her time here."

"How's her little boy?"

"Good. I'll tell her you asked about her and Harry." We watched the ocean for a few minutes and then I got up. "I better get back to work. I should give Annie an update."

"Have a nice day, Nathan."

"You, too, Ms. June." When I got to the end of the ramp off the boardwalk, I turned to look at Ms. June. She had gotten up and started stretching. I grinned at the thought that for an old lady, she was pretty spry. She then leaned over and I got an eyeful. I think my retinas were burned with the bright yellow image.

I entered the building into an empty lobby. I went to press the elevator button but headed to the mailboxes. I discarded the items addressed to 'current resident'. The only item of note was from the managing agent of the condo. They hadn't received her payment yet. All her other bills she had set up to be paid regularly online. This payment required a check. I didn't want to burden Annie with it and decided I would pay it myself. I'd feel less guilty about sleeping on her couch.

I sat in the lobby with pictures of Lily to ask her neighbors if they had seen anything unusual. Anyone who had lived in the building for over ten years recognized "Genevieve." Most of the newer residents didn't recognize her at all. I had a picture of Lily with Laude and everyone recognized Laude. No one had anything useful to say. I was getting frustrated by the ambivalence of her disappearance.

Gregory Straub arrived after five, carrying a box from Rein's bakery. I recognized him from the many photos Mrs. Straub had in her apartment.

I showed him the picture of Lily and he shrugged. He proceeded to the elevator. "Wait, what about this one?" He looked at the picture of Laude. "That's Laude. Oh, is that her dog?"

"Yes, it's her dog. And you already know that."

"Excuse me?"

"You told your mother how much you liked Lillian's dog. How much did you like Laude? How much did you like Lillian?"

"Excuse me?" he repeated. "I really have to go see my mother."

"If you have her, I will find her. If you hurt her, I have no idea what I'll do to you." I said as the elevator doors closed.

LILY

Tuesday   March 10, 2009

I couldn't wait to get back to work with the knife. As soon as Craig left, I got off the bed and turned to Laude. 'This is it girl. We're getting out today." Her ears perked up and her head tilted to the side. I took a deep breath, took the knife out of the bedside table. I pulled the bedside table over to the 'window.' It took me three hours to pull out the remaining nails. I took a deep breath when I removed the final nail and lowered the plywood to the ground.

The good news was the awful picture of the ocean was down. The bad news was there was no window behind it.

For weeks I had pictured a small basement window behind that plywood, like the ones that my parents had in their basement. I pictured trying to open the window and when I found it locked, breaking it with whatever I could. I would then make sure all the shards of glass were clear and place Laude through it. I'd give her a strict sit verbal and hand command which she would obey. Finally, I would have climbed out and then run for help. These vivid images came courtesy of all the thrillers I read.

I had fantasized this escape during the hours I had laid awake last night. For nothing. All that lay on the other side of the plywood was a brick wall.

I lay on the bed for an hour after my disappointment. I had to decide what to do with the plywood. I was a bit overzealous with the last few nails and I couldn't put it back up. I pulled the shade down, and put the plywood under the bed. I didn't think he'd notice. Just like many times before, I was wrong.

After Laude's walk, I heard his voice through the walls, "I see you've done some remodeling."

"I needed some Vitamin D." I had placed a pillow over the speaker and didn't think he could see me anymore.

"I understand. You are a little pale." That was an understatement. I was pale before I had been locked in a basement for three weeks.

"I'm sorry you were disappointed." I'm sure he wasn't. "I'll admit the picture wasn't so great either." Another understatement.

"Nope." I was too tired to be polite. "It's under the bed if you want it."

"You tried your best."

"I did." I wasn't sure if he meant I tried my best to live with it or to hide it or to get it off the wall. My head hurt trying to figure him out. Yep, it was like we were really dating.

NATHAN

Tuesday   March 10, 2009

I knew I should have called Annie yesterday but I had nothing to report so I delayed it. On the way home, after work, I finally did.

"Nathan, how are you?," she answered, ever hopeful.

I knew she didn't want to know how I was. She just wanted to know if I had made any progress.

"Fine. You?"

"Fine." My father used to say 'fine' was a four letter word. He knew that whenever mom said she was fine, she wasn't. It seemed the most appropriate answer for both Annie and myself today.

"I went to see Florence yesterday."

I could hear Annie's breathing so I knew she was still there. But that was the only way I knew.

"She doesn't know anything about Lily. She hasn't seen or talked to her in months."

Nothing. I continued, "She wasn't friendly. She didn't seem concerned."

"I don't know, Nathan. It's so odd. I know how much she loved Lily. Are you sure you didn't confuse her unfriendliness as depression? Maybe she's just withdrawn, can't deal with it all."

"She slammed the door in my face."

"That sounds more like Charlie than Florence." I could hear the tension in her voice. When I had met Annie in her home, she called

Florence, 'Aunt Florence'. I wasn't surprised that the 'aunt' moniker had been dropped.

"Charlie?"

"Florence's son. I've only met him a few times. None of them pleasant."

"How do you mean?"

"Basically, he's a drunk. He's unemployed. All around, a loser." She took a deep breath and continued, "I was always surprised that Charlie was her son. Chloe, her daughter, is nice but I met her even less." Annie had started out angry but now she was beginning to cry. "But what do I know? I thought Florence was the best aunt possible. And now she doesn't even care that Lily is missing?" I could hear her trying to say more but she couldn't get it out through the sobs.

"Don't worry, Annie. I'll keep looking. She's out there. I'll find her."

Annie tried to say something that sounded like agreement and then she hung up.

We ended our last conversation the same way as the last time, with Annie in tears. She was so disappointed that the video surveillance had yielded nothing.

Before I realized what I was doing, I was driving to Long Beach again, to Lily's.

One of my roommates in college had been a computer science major. He had shown me a few tricks through that year. Days ago, I had given Lily's computer a thorough review and found nothing. Her web history didn't show anything unusual. Her phone and bank accounts showed no activity after February 13th. In the months since Lily had opened the accounts, there were no suspicious withdrawals or deposits.

The only thing I didn't check was her credit report. If, as Steve had believed, Lily had picked up and started a new life somewhere else, a credit check would reveal it. It, too, showed nothing. Part of me was disappointed; a bigger part of me was relieved. I didn't know how I would have reacted if I had seen credit checks for an apartment or a new job in a new city. I should have been happy to have found her; to know she was safe. But, a Lily who had decided to start a new life without telling anyone would not have been the Lily I knew.

NATHAN

Thursday   March 12, 2009

"He's the only suspect I have," I told Steve after we ordered our beers and burgers at Sammie's. He'd pointed out I owed him a drink, so I thought I'd throw in dinner too to get more help with Lily.

"Suspect? Because he liked her dog?"

"The mother said he's been acting differently. He's a big guy. He could have carried her out. He knows the building. He has keys. No one would have noticed him."

"No one who would have noticed him carrying a yelling woman out of the building?"

"He took her out via the stairs. Had to. No cameras in the garage or stairwells."

"If he liked her, why wouldn't he just ask her out?"

"Maybe he did and she said no. And that set him off. He has had a restraining order against another woman right?'

"Yes."

"And he's been staying somewhere else. His mother said she has never seen it. He hasn't changed his address. It's still listed as Mrs. Straub's, which Tony said is against condo policy."

"Lots of people move into a condo without getting approval. And plenty of people do not change their address on their driver's license in a timely manner."

Our orders came and he blew off any other attempts I made to discuss Lillian. We ate in silence.

NATHAN

Friday   March 13, 2009

"Nathan!," Mrs Straub yelled as I was leaving the building to get breakfast.

"Yes, Mrs. Straub." I expected her to say something about my run in with her son.

She was smiling. "I can't find Tony. And my son won't be coming by today. He has 'plans.'" It didn't appear he had mentioned meeting me earlier in the week.

I stood waiting for more information. "Could you help me move my dresser? Something fell behind it."

"Of course." It would give me an opportunity to learn more about Gregory.

"So, your son has plans tonight?" I asked as I followed her onto the elevator.

She rambled on about Gregory as we headed to her apartment. She initially sounded annoyed that Gregory wasn't available to help her but then sounded happy that he wasn't sulking in her home anymore.

I followed her into the bedroom and she pointed to the dresser she needed moved to get what had fallen behind it. She started clearing items off of it- her jewelry box, a few picture frames and a figurine. I picked the figurine up and examined it closely. My heart was racing. The female character was running towards home plate, towards a trunk with a wedding dress. Turning it over, it was stamped "Precious Moments." I was sure it was the one Annie had described. Discreetly, I took a picture of it on my cell phone and texted it to Annie, with "Is this it? Call me ASAP!" I placed it on the bed carefully, not wanting to break the evidence I had.

"Where'd you get this ma'am?"

"My son gave it to me."

"Really?" I couldn't suppress my smile. "When?"

"Mom?" I heard Gregory yell as he entered the apartment. "Mom, I got your message about dropping your insurance card. Mom?" he yelled again before entering the bedroom. "What the hell are you doing in here?," he said once he saw me. He ran up to his mother. "Are you alright?"

"Of course I am. Nathan said he'd help me get the card."

"Your mom and I were just talking about this figurine." I held it out to him. "Where'd you get it, Gregory?"

I glared at him. He glared back.

"I'm sorry. Gregory, have you met Nathan?"

"Yes," he answered curtly.

She looked back and forth between us, curious of why we were staring at each other.

"He's looking for the lady with that dog you like."

"Yes, I know. He thinks I had something to do with it."

"Where were you February 13th?" I asked.

"What?" she yelled. "Why would he think that?"

He ignored my question, answering his mother instead. "I have no idea."

"The restraining order is the obvious reason." I said.

"What? What is he talking about, *Gregory*? *A restraining order?*"

He ignored his mother this time. "That weekend I was in Atlantic City for a friend's bachelor party. Plenty of witnesses. Those casinos have plenty of video proof, too."

And I looked forward to disproving his fabricated alibi. I smiled when I heard my phone beep, signaling a text. I glanced at the phone and was disheartened to read- "That's not it. It doesn't have the chip." I hung my head in defeat.

"And I met my girlfriend that weekend," he continued.

"*A girlfriend?,*" Mrs. Straub cried.

He pulled out his phone, showing pictures of the boys' weekend, while his mother stood next to him, hands across her chest, with increasing anger. The pictures were clearly from Valentine's Day weekend, with the prevalence of red and hearts decor in the background.

I avoided an awkward exit because his mother was yelling about a restraining order and a girlfriend she knew nothing about.

LILY

Friday   March 13, 2009

I was dozing on the bed when I heard the awful high pitched beep. I opened my eyes and looked around. Minutes later, it beeped again. Laude jumped off the bed and cowered in the corner.

"It's ok, Laude. I'll get it." It was the smoke detector beep signaling it needed a new battery. I stood on the bed and fiddled with it, trying to figure out how to shut it off.

It beeped again. It was an awful sound. I cringed at the thought of having to listen to it for hours until Craig came home. I looked over at Laude and knew she agreed. Her ears were down and she was shaking. She ran from the corner and hid under the bed.

I couldn't find the latch for the battery like my old smoke detector had. I fiddled some more and it came unhinged from the part attached to the ceiling. I could only imagine my shocked face as I saw what was inside. Craig wouldn't have to imagine. He'd see it.

I had known there was a camera in the bedroom since the first week. I didn't know it was the smoke detector. I never even suspected it.

I had moved around the room assuming the camera was in the speaker in the right corner of the room. I had become accustomed to dressing and undressing in the bathroom. Other than watching television, I didn't think the camera could see me. Craig hadn't mentioned seeing me anymore so I figured he didn't see anything worth noting when he watched the video. I should have known when he didn't say anything about the pillow blocking the view that the speaker didn't have a camera.

What bothered me most was this was the same smoke detector in my home. The new ones I thought Tony had put in my bedroom and living room in January. But I knew now it wasn't Tony who put them there.

Laude came out from under the bed. Happy to have the beeping stopped, she ran around with her toy squeaking in her mouth. So this was how Craig knew all about me and my life. But how did he get in my apartment in the first place?

At least the beeping had stopped.

I heard him come down the stairs after work. I was lying on the bed watching the news. Instead of opening the doggie door as Laude waited patiently on our side of it, he knocked and slowly opened the door.

He sheepishly said, "Sorry about the camera." I wasn't sure if he meant sorry I found it or sorry he had ever put it up. I had nothing to say.

"I'll fix it." I looked up at him. He added, "Without the camera." He held my gaze.

I decided guilt was my best course of action. "It just concerns me that you keep me in a room with no smoke detector."

"Oh no, it works too. It's a functioning smoke detector as well as a camera." He sounded proud. "Doing double duty really eats up the batteries fast. Your safety and Laude's safety are my highest priority." I found that ironic. "Come on. You believe me. I even put the carbon monoxide monitor up." He looked away from me and wiped his eyes. It was first time he openly admitted to being in my home.

He cleared his throat. "I know how important that is." He placed the new smoke detector box on the bed and opened it. He pulled out the new one and I watched as he opened it to put in a new battery. I didn't see a camera but he could have just purchased a better one. I took the box and turned it over. It looked like a real smoke detector with only one purpose.

"Is this the only camera you have in here?" I didn't add "and in Long Beach" figuring the answer would be the same. He turned to me, not understanding the question. "Do you have any cameras anywhere else? Like..." and I motioned to the bathroom.

Craig looked horrified. "Of course not. And I looked away anytime you were indecent."

Partially relieved that my stalker had only watched me when I was 'decent', I leaned back onto the pillow and watched him work. He finished and surveyed the room. "Pretty amazing right? I was able to get everything just like your place."

I nodded agreement.

"I was so busy getting your room ready, I didn't even watch too much of the tapes right before you got here." He talked as if I was an honored houseguest and not a prisoner. "I finished it that Thursday. I was so happy when you moved up our date."

Not watching the last few days did explain how he didn't hear me arguing with Annie about the blind date. He had no clue that Annie had impersonated me on the website. I didn't know how he'd react to that.

He walked over to the dresser and picked up the Precious Moments figurine. "Except this. Couldn't find it anywhere! So I just took it when I got Laude. I knew you'd notice if it wasn't here. Wouldn't be 'home' without it." He smiled, proud of himself and the pun with the figurines name, "Running towards home."

I looked around for Laude. Laude was sitting patiently by the open bedroom door. He had us both trained well. We both could and should run. I knew if I ran, Craig would catch me before I got halfway up the stairs. Unless, I could detain him somehow.

While Craig continued with putting up the new smoke detector, I looked around the room for something I could use to throw at him. There was nothing.

My best bet was to lock him in the bathroom. I could use the nightstand to block the door and then run.

"While you're down here, the toilet is running. Can you fix it?" I asked.

"No, it's not."

Surprised, I asked, "I'm sorry?" I thought getting him into the bathroom would be the easy part of the plan. Keeping him in there was going to be the difficult part.

"The toilet's not running, Lillian."

I got off the bed in preparation for grabbing the nightstand. "Well, sure, now its not but it does after I use it," I explained.

My heart dropped with his answer, "Lillian," and accompanying intent glare.

"I know you better than you think," he said as he left the room with Laude for their evening walk. I sat back on the bed, head in my hands, as I heard the door lock behind them.

LILY

Monday   March 16, 2009

In college I learned that it takes three to six weeks to form a habit. I was pleased with myself that it had only taken a day to get into a regular habit of exercise. Three weeks later, I was still sticking to it. I would do two or three workout shows daily. I think I had a bit more motivation than most. The boredom helped too. There was only so much television I could watch.

I laughed that maybe I could give Ms. June a run for her money now. She was in pretty good shape so maybe not. "This would be more entertaining if I had one of Ms. June's colorful outfits on, right?" Laude was running around with her toy and didn't acknowledge me.

I had always been a fairly punctual person; Craig was too. I had little to guide my day except the television and Craig's comings and goings. Weekdays, he took Laude out at seven, shortly afterwards I would hear his car leave. I rarely heard anything else until he returned at five. Then, he would take Laude out again. Before eleven, Laude would have her final walk of the day. On weekends, the routine was basically the same. Sometimes, I'd hear him leave the house. Sometimes, I wouldn't. I never heard anyone else. I spent one day shouting and banging on the wall in the hopes a passerby, a mailman maybe, would hear me. I had nothing to show for it but a raspy voice and bruised fists the next several days.

I never thought much of his routine until he alternated from it. It was the most scared I had been since the first day.

At five past five, I noticed he was late.

At fifteen past five, Laude noticed he was late. She was sitting at the door. She would look at the door and then look back at me.

At twenty past, she started whimpering. I tried to soothe her but when you have to go, you have to go. I put her in the bathtub. I wasn't sure how Craig would react if she had an accident on the carpet. I was always afraid of what little thing would break his tenuous grasp on reality. If she went to the bathroom in the bathtub, I could clean it without any difficulty.

At five thirty, I was trying not to panic. I knew I was dependent on him. He provided us with food. Before I realized it, I was pacing the length of the room. It felt more like a cell than it had ever felt before. What would happen if he didn't come home? We would die of starvation in this space.

At five forty five, Laude was scratching at the bathroom door and she was crying again. I should have known the tub wouldn't contain her for long. I opened the door to try to quiet her and she bolted past me. Within a minute, I heard Craig's car. Laude started barking. Craig came running down the stairs, repeating, "I'm sorry, Laude."

They ran upstairs after he unlocked the doggy door.

I didn't think I was ever so relieved to hear someone home.

NATHAN

Tuesday   10 p.m.   March 17, 2009

I was looking at my notes when I heard the ding of the elevator. Having always lived in a one family dwelling, all the little noises of apartment living captured my attention. I'm sure after living here a while you got used to it.

I went back to my notes but still could hear someone walking down the hall. He, or she, seemed to be making a lot of noise. The noise stopped outside my door. Lily's door. There was a rattling of keys. The keys fell. There was a groan as the person picked them up. I hadn't met the person across the hall and debated if this was the right time to meet him or her. The keys jingled again. I heard mumbling then I heard the person trying to open my door. I got up and opened it for them.

Part of me thought I would see Lillian. I didn't realize how large a part of me until I was disappointed to find a man there.

He had to be close to forty five. His dark hair was disheveled, like the rest of him. He reeked of alcohol and cigarettes. As the door opened, he dropped the keys again and grabbed the door jam to steady himself. He looked up at me, stunned that the door was opened. His eyes were bloodshot.

"Who the fuck are you?," he asked.

I didn't have to ask who he was because I knew it had to be Charlie. I did anyway.

"I'm Charlie McGowan." His further rant was interrupted by a belch. "This is my place." Charlie must have visited a few of the local bars to celebrate St. Patrick's Day.

"No, it isn't. This is Genevieve's place."

"Genevieve, that little bitch. Precious Genevieve. Mom loved that bitch. She told me she's gone so this place is mine." He tried to come in but I blocked the doorway.

"No, she's just missing. Plus, if she is really," I hesitated. I couldn't get myself to say dead, "gone, it goes to whoever she bequeaths it to." I knew that wasn't him. And I knew he didn't know what 'bequeaths' meant. Even sober, Charlie wouldn't understand anything but monosyllabic words. He tried to look at me, but his eyes barely focused. "Who ever she willed it to," I answered before he could ask.

He seemed to understand that. "And that would be me." He tried to get in again.

"I doubt that," I mumbled. "Well, I'm housesitting for her. I'll have her give you a call when she comes home." I started to close the door but he blocked it.

"I think it's time you went home," I told him.

"This is my home."

"No. This is Lily's home."

"No, this is my home." This would last hours or until Charlie passed out. We were in a stalemate. I wasn't letting him in and he wasn't leaving.

I reached into my pocket and got my cell phone out. Steve answered with a grunt before the second ring. He was never happy to be working St. Patrick's night. This was only going to make it worse.

"Need some help here. The cousin is here, drunk."

"And where is 'here'?"

"I think you know."

"Should I guess?"

"Really, not the time, Steve."

"Be right over."

Five minutes later, Steve was getting off the elevator. A few of the neighbors were out. Charlie was on the floor now. He had gradually slid down and now had his back against the doorjamb. His legs were splayed across the hallway. Ms. June was among the gawkers.

"Charlie, why don't you just go home?," she asked him. I was guessing this wasn't the first time she had seen Charlie drunk.

His speech was becoming more garbled. "Why don't you mind your own business, you nosy old bitch?"

Steve said, "Time to get going, ..." and looked up at me.

"Charlie" I filled in for him.

At the sound of his name, he looked up at me. "Nope, this is my home."

"No, I know it is not. If you don't leave, I'm going to have to arrest you," Steve told him. Charlie chose being arrested.

In a normal family, Charlie would have been the black sheep, not Lily.

NATHAN

Wednesday   March 18, 2009

I called Annie in the morning.

"How are you, Annie?"

"Fine. Anything new?" She always sounded so hopeful when I called. But we both knew that if she got the good news she wanted, she'd be talking to Lily, not me.

"I met Charlie last night."

"That must have been fun. He's a real piece of work."

"You're right."

"Did you go see him? You don't think he had something to do with Lily disappearing, do you?"

"No. He came to see me."

"What? Why?," she asked, shocked.

"He was claiming his property. He's pretty angry that the apartment isn't his."

"I'm sure he is." Her surprise was gone.

"Why would you think he had anything to do with Lily disappearing?," I asked her.

"No, I don't. I don't think Lily's even seen him since the funeral. They were never close and he was pretty odd at the funeral. He was more upset about his car than his aunt and uncle being dead."

"What was wrong with his car?"

"I don't know. He just kept pestering Aunt Florence about buying him a new one."

There was a lengthy silence. I wished I could tell her something positive. Every phone call had me asking more questions that didn't seem to get me any closer to finding Lily.

"I'm sorry I don't have anything else to tell you."

"One of these days you will."

I wasn't sure if she was trying to convince me or herself.

NATHAN

Thursday   March 19, 2009

I visited Steve at the police department two days after Charlie's arrest. I came on the pretext of thanking him but really wanted information on Charlie.

He was at his desk, filling out paperwork.

"Hey, Steve. Thanks for the other night." I handed him a cup of coffee.

"Thanks," he said as he accepted the cup. "And you're welcome." He took a sip and gestured for me to sit. "That guy's something. His blood alcohol was off the charts."

"Agreed. That does seem to be the consensus. Bad enough the aunt didn't care that Lily was gone, but he was actually glad."

"You want to see his arrest history." He handed me a few sheets of paper.

He got to the point quicker than I expected. "Thanks."

"Didn't think you came all this way just to say thanks."

"I did bring you coffee, buddy."

I looked through his arrests, a couple of drunk and dis-orderlies and a few DUIs. I wasn't surprised. Then, I had a thought that did surprise me.

When I got to work, I looked up the car history of Charles McGowan. He was forty years old and had owned three cars in the last four years. His current car was a black Jeep. His last car was a red Mustang.

I called a friend at the Pennsylvania State Troopers. After catching up, I told him I was working on a case and asked for the report on the car crash of Wally and Beverly Brannon. It was the truth. I left out that I wasn't working on the case officially. Professional courtesy, he sent it.

There wasn't much information in the report. Wally and Beverly were dead when the first officer arrived. It was believed they died on impact. They had been traveling south on the county road that led to the college. It was late, about ten at night, when the trooper arrived. Based on when they left the breeder to get Laude and when they were found in a ditch off the road, it was believed the crash occurred between 8:30pm and 9:30pm.

The investigation found skid marks from the Brannon's car. Red markings and dents were on the driver's side. There were no skid marks coming from the other side. There were no witnesses available. No witnesses that could speak that is, only Laude. The report was inconclusive.

I called Keith back to review the report, hoping to find out something not in it.

When I reminded him where the accident occurred, he told me many accidents had occurred there over the past few years. There was a bar two miles down the road and there had a been a few drunk driving accidents along the winding route.

I heard him rifle through some papers and he mumbled some of the reports findings as he read it.

"Oh, yeah. I remember this now. Graduation weekend is always busy there. They had a daughter graduating. Real sad. The investigating officer thought a red sports car had driven them off the road. According to the family, the Brannon's car was in good condition before the crash. No previous accidents. Those dents, with the red paint, were new. He couldn't find any conclusive proof and couldn't put it in the report. Just conjecture."

Charlie had a red sports car, that was no longer available to him on May 26. Lily and Annie never knew what happened to it. Maybe Lillian had put it together too. Maybe that was why she was gone. Charlie didn't have a history of violence but maybe when forced with the truth he did.

It was the first break I had.

NATHAN

Saturday   March 21, 2009

I went to see Charlie. I pulled up to his apartment in Mineola. It was a non-descript, two story building. Poorly maintained, its white paint was faded and chipped. I knocked on the door several times before anyone answered. Then Charlie appeared, looking at me as if he had never seen me before. He looked as he did on St. Patrick's Day night, disheveled, and he smelled the same too. As courteous as ever, he said "What?"

"May I come in, Charlie?"

"Who are you?" He continued to block the doorway. In this position, he resembled his mother.

"Nathan." The less information I gave him the better.

He squinted trying to get a better look at me. "Do I know you?" His posture relaxed as he tilted his head, leaning it against the door.

"We've met," I answered.

"Sure, come in." He stepped aside, revealing an equally disheveled home. There were clothes, dirty dishes, and liquor bottles strewn all over. I walked over to the chair with the least amount of items on it and sat down.

"So, how are you, Nate?" I smiled at him calling me Nate. Some guys shortened names automatically. Fellow cops did it all the time. When I first joined the force, I made the mistake of correcting a senior officer that my name was Nathan, not Nate. It was a mistake that I only made once. Fortunately, most called me "Mic." With Charlie, I was going to let it go. If he told me what I wanted to know, he could call me anything he wanted.

"Pretty good. You?"

"Fine."

"Heard you got arrested again."

"Yep. I went over to my cousin's. Damn place should be mine. Think I passed out in the hallway. Someone called the cops."

Even with the prompting of how we met, he didn't remember me. It made me wonder what else he didn't remember.

"How'd her folks die again?" I had planned on idle chit chat for a bit but he opened the door with the mention of his cousin so I dove right in.

"Car crash. They were good people. She's a little brat. My mom gave her the apartment afterwards." He took a swig of some clear alcohol from the bottle. I was guessing vodka was today's drink of choice. Looking around, it appeared his drinking taste varied. Beer cans, vodka bottles, scotch bottles. All the cheapest brands. Charlie chose quantity over quality.

"Where were you?," I asked.

"When?"

"When they died."

"I don't know. At some bar. Mom woke me up the next day to tell me." He took another long swallow.

I thought the more alcohol he drank, the more cooperative he'd be, up to a point.

"I'm sorry man." He held out the bottle to me. "You want something to drink?" I shook my head no. "I got some cold ones in the fridge," pointing to the kitchen.

"Sure." He didn't make any effort to get up. I got up and got a beer. The same mess extended into the kitchen. Bottles, empty and half empty, and dishes, all dirty, were on the counter. The refrigerator had a sour smell, a six pack, and little else. I grabbed a beer and returned to the living room. Charlie appeared to have passed out. I debated looking around when I tripped and kicked one of the empty bottles. Charlie stirred. "Hey, man."

"How's the new car working out?," I asked trying to keep the conversation going.

"Pretty good."

"You must miss that sweet Mustang."

He perked up at the mention of his old car. "Sure do. Had some engine, a V8, in it. But the Jeep's good. Better in this weather." More snow was forecasted, adding to the six inches that had fallen yesterday.

"Guess so. I'd rather have the Mustang myself." Charlie shrugged his shoulders and took another drink.

"Who'd you sell it to?"

He shrugged. "Somewhere in Pennsylvania. My mom sold it. Told me I couldn't drive it, a little banged up or something. She got me that Jeep."

"Oh that sweet ride. Too bad."

"Yea, too bad." Charlie looked like he was fading again.

"How'd it get banged up?"

"Don't know." His eyes closed again and didn't reopen. He started snoring. I retraced my steps carefully avoiding any bottles. I wanted to get out before Charlie woke up again.

I needed to speak to Florence. But I knew she wouldn't talk to me willingly. She was a tough lady but I knew her weakness.

A different security guard opened the gate when I showed my badge. It was my lucky day. There was another front desk lady on duty as well. She was talking, that is to say flirting, with one of the male employees. I walked in and no one noticed me. I went up to Florence's room and knocked on the door. "Who is it?"

"Nathan."

She paused, then opened the door. She was clearly surprised to see me again. "What the hell do you want? I told you I didn't know anything. I told you to leave." To herself she added, "I had better security at the condo. No one got in there that I didn't want to."

"I'm here about Charlie." She stared at me, hands on her hips. "I'm sure you heard about his most recent arrest."

"Of course I did. Who the hell do you think bailed him out? Again, that's not you're jurisdiction. And none of your business."

"It is when I was the one who called the cops." She continued to stare. "And my friend made the arrest."

A pair of old ladies were walking past and both looked our way when they heard 'arrest'. Florence moved aside, signaling me in.

"Let's make this quick. Bingo's in fifteen minutes." It was a small apartment. Smaller than the one she had owned in Long Beach. She sat at the small dining table. It only had two chairs. I sat across from her.

We sat there for a minute glaring at each other. "Charlie's got quite the rap sheet," I pointed out.

"He's had his problems," she answered.

"Mostly with alcohol."

"Yes."

"At least he didn't hurt anyone this time."

"He has no history of hurting anyone." She didn't break eye contact.

"No official history of hurting anyone, you mean." And then she did.

"I think it's time for you to leave." She stood up and headed for the door.

"We're not done yet." She continued to the door. "I know." She stopped, but kept her back to me.

"NO, you think you know. If you could prove what you thought you knew then we'd be in a police department right now." She turned and smirked at me.

"True, I might not be able to prove it in a court of law but I do know that *your* son ran *your* sister and her husband off the road, killing them both. And *you* covered it up." She looked towards the window. She walked over to it and watched the passing cars.

"How could you do this?," I asked.

"I'm not admitting anything."

"You covered everything up and then abandoned Genevieve."

"Abandoned Genevieve! I did everything for her. I gave her my home. I moved into this this..." She paused trying to find the words "...this purgatory!"

"He doesn't even know. Does he?"

"No." It had been a hunch. Florence was right. I had no real evidence. I had nothing that would hold up in court. But, I was right. My gut told me the red car and their suspicious behavior afterwards were connected.

"Did he hurt Genevieve?"

She turned and glared at me. "No. Why would he do that?"

"He's pretty mad about that condo. He's very angry that you gave it to Genevieve. That condo's a lot nice than the place he's living. Maybe he went over another time and got rid of her. Then the place would be his. Did you help him cover that up too?"

"*No. I did not.*" She looked truly shocked that I would ask.

"Did Genevieve learn what you two did? Is that why she's missing?" I tried to keep my volume down but was unsuccessful.

She looked back out the window and softly said, "No. She didn't know." I believed her.

"When was the last time you saw her?"

"Like I told you last time, I have not seen or talked to her since November."

"Sorry for not believing you. You haven't proven yourself to be a reliable witness." I said sarcastically. "Did you hurt Genevieve?"

"No."

"That's where you're wrong. You and your son may not have physically hurt her but you caused her some serious damage. Not only did she lose her parents that night, but she lost the rest of her family too." I cleared my throat and continued, "And she has no idea why."

"And you don't think I lost anything! I lost *my* family! My sister Bev. My baby girl Genevieve. *How much have I lost?*" She briskly wiped away the tears that had started to fall. "You've made your point. And you can't do a damn thing about it. *Just get out,*" she yelled.

And I did.

I had inadvertently solved the mystery of why Florence had stopped talking to her niece. But I was no closer to finding Lily.

To confirm that Florence had nothing to do with Lily's disappearance I stopped by the administration office. I walked over to the bulletin board to see pictures from the community's Valentine's Day party, held February 13, 2009 and Valentine's Day brunch with family on February 14, 2009. Florence was in a few of them, hanging in the edges. Never with a smile on her face.

The administrator's assistant confirmed Florence hadn't left the facility that weekend. She then looked around to see if anyone was listening. "That son of hers came by too. He came to the party on Friday. We had to get security to take him home he was so drunk. Not the first time either."

I doubted it would be the last time.

I headed back to my home. My home in Queens. Not the apartment that I had made my home more nights than I should have in Long Beach. As I approached my door, I looked around at the neighborhood.

Was I much different from Lily in my daily life? How long would I be gone before someone noticed? Before someone did something to find me? I spoke to my mom once a week. I spoke to my sisters every couple of weeks. I spoke to friends sporadically. I was staying at Lily's a lot and no one had noticed.

LILY

Monday   March 23, 2009

When Laude returned from her evening walk, she had a note attached to her collar "Anniversary Wednesday - Special night! Pick you up at 7 p.m." Looking back, I wondered if he regretted calling it a 'special night.'

I had enough time to put a few things together in the six weeks I'd been here. The anniversary was Christmas. He had seen me on Christmas. I figured it was that evening while Laude and I had sat on one of the benches on the boardwalk for awhile.

I started to cry when I realized that if Aunt Florence was still speaking to me this would have never happened. I would have been at her home, or Chloe's, or worse case, my home. I could have cooked for all of them. Annie would have laughed at the thought of me cooking Christmas dinner. It made me cry even harder.

I was determined to make March 25 a special night.

LILY

Wednesday   March 25, 2009

I was running out of options. I had no idea how long he would keep me here. My tunneling out plan was going very slowly. Actually, it was going nowhere. I had tried the front door and the back door during my previous escape attempts. I had seen enough slasher flicks to know not to run upstairs.

I saw only one way I hadn't tried. The window.

I wore the clothes from our second date. The sweater, jeans and boots provided me with the most skin coverage and protection.

Craig smiled when he saw me. He started to lean in towards me, as if he was going to kiss me, but stopped. He handed me a box of chocolates instead. My mouth watered at the sight. I couldn't remember the last time I had chocolate. Craig interuppted my thoughts of ripping into the box, "Dinner first, Lillian." He reached down and patted Laude's head. "Sorry, none for you, girl." She ran up the stairs and he followed her.

I smiled as I watched him walk up the stairs. He was thoughtful. I had never dated a man who remembered anniversaries. Annie's husband, Jeffrey, was a good man but I had to remind him about Annie's birthday and their anniversary. Usually more than once.

I stopped myself, realizing how I had thought of Craig- as a man I dated. I needed to get out of here. I ran to catch up to Craig at the top of the stairs, pleased that I wasn't winded.

Not looking at the window, not wanting to give away my plan, I walked to my chair and sat in my chair. I folded my hands across my lap to keep them from shaking. The adrenaline was pumping and my heart was beating as if I'd run a mile.

"I'll be right back," he said, as he pushed my chair in.

As the door to the kitchen swung closed behind Craig, I signaled Laude over to me. Still seated, I picked her up and put her on the table. As quickly as I could, I picked up the chair and threw it out the window. I had the irrational thought that the further I threw it, the lower the chair alarm would sound. Of course, that was true but I think the glass shattering gave me away.

Laude stood on the table and watched me as I grabbed a napkin to wrap around my right hand. I grabbed Laude with my left and punched out the remaining shards of glass. I climbed out the window as I heard the swinging door slam against the wall. I didn't turn to see Craig come back into the room. I imagined his shocked face as he saw me climbing out the dining room window.

My sweater snagged on some remaining glass. I felt nothing but fresh, cold air on my face. The higher than expected jump out the window jarred my knees but couldn't stop me. I screamed and ran with Laude in my arms. I could see the street and ran as fast I could.

But Craig ran faster.

When he caught me, I was about twenty feet from the house. I fell to the ground. I wasn't sure if I lost my balance or if my knees had given out when he grabbed me. I was lying on my left side and could see the front door was wide open. He had taken the less adventurous way out of the house.

He gently touched my shoulder. "If you needed some fresh air, you could have just asked." Our eyes met and I was afraid what I would see there. I expected rage but he looked at me calmly. Laude wiggled out of my arms and starting running around. I hoped she would run to the next house and bark for help. But, Lassie she was not.

I took a deep breath. For a few glorious seconds, I had been free. I thought I had escaped. I had made it only a few feet more than the failed attempt out the back door. I had no words, just tears.

"Why are you crying? Oh no. You're bleeding." He picked me up and carried me into the house. Laude ran around his feet, barking the whole time. I looked over Craig's shoulder and could see two houses- one across the street and one to the right. Both had lights on but no one came out to see what the ruckus was.

He closed the front door behind us and proceeded to the kitchen. He placed me on the floor against the wall. "I'll be right back. Try to hold your arm up."

I heard him run upstairs. If I had any energy this would be the time to run, but I was spent. Blood from my right arm was beginning to pool on the floor.

As I heard him running down the stairs, I feared this would be the moment when he would finally snap- blood all over his pristine floor.

I had seen it in the nursing homes. The dementia patients who were 'pleasantly confused.' They would be so sweet and then the smallest thing would set them off. It would take time, and sometimes medication, to settle them back down. I had neither.

Craig returned with first aid supplies. He looked calm but worried. I hoped he was worried that neighbors had heard the commotion and had called the police.

His hands shook as he placed the supplies next to me. He swept his ever lightening colored hair, now light brown, away from his eyes. "You would probably be better with this than me. You've taken first aid classes, right?"

"Yes, I have." The small talk reminded me of how my mom would distract me if I had a splinter.

Craig held several gauze pads against the outside of my upper arm and we watched as they went from white to crimson. He took them off and inspected the wound before placing new gauze on it. "Don't worry. I think we just need to stop the bleeding. No stitches."

I didn't trust his judgement about the stitches. If I needed them, would he take me? I doubted it but maybe he would. Times like this made me think he actually cared about me. I had thought that too many times over the past few weeks. I was becoming a possible subject for a study on Stockholm syndrome.

Maybe that would be my next escape plan- injure myself to the need of hospitalization. I wasn't sure if I wanted to test that possibility.

Laude sat against my left side as Craig tenderly applied pressure to the wound. I slowly slouched lower on the wall. Eventually he helped me lie flat on the kitchen floor. When the bleeding stopped, he poured alcohol over the wound. I cringed from the stinging and Laude growled.

"Don't worry Laude. She'll be just fine." He leaned in and closely looked at the wound. "No glass in it. That's good." I closed my eyes and debated if he was talking to himself or me. He placed a gauze pad over the cut and wrapped it to keep it in place.

I heard him repackage his supplies and go upstairs. Laude stayed at my side. I'm not sure how long he was gone.

When he came back in, he asked "Lil, are you o.k.?" It was a loaded question and there were too many ways to answer it. Lying on the floor with a large gash in my arm, being held hostage in a basement, no I was not "O.K." I just wanted to keep my eyes closed and go to sleep. I hoped I'd wake up somewhere else.

He crept closer and knelt next to me. "Lillian?"

"Yes." I opened my eyes to find him just inches from my face. Again, he seemed genuinely concerned. "I'd like to go to bed now." I tried to get up by myself but Craig took my left hand and boosted me up. I was unsteady but walked to the basement stairs. His arm was around my waist and Laude was at my heel. He opened the door and kept his arm around my waist as we went down the stairs. At the bottom of the stairs, Laude ran ahead and jumped on the bed.

I started to climb into bed to join her. Craig stopped me. "You have to get out of those clothes, Lillian." He hesitated before adding, "You're a bit of a mess." I looked down and saw he was right. I was covered in blood and dirt. Before I could object, he helped me out of my clothes and into pajamas. He lifted the comforter and I crawled in. My eyes were closed before I hit the pillow.

He tucked me in and kissed me on the top of my head. "I love you, Lillian."

I didn't know if I was woozy from the blood loss or just weary from the last few weeks but I believed him.

That was the last time I tried to escape. I had run out of options anyway. The next day I would run out of desire to escape.

LILY

Thursday   March 26, 2009

"I love you, Lillian" was the last thing I clearly remembered of the night before. I didn't remember hearing him leave or the door being locked. I was afraid to open my eyes and find him still in the room. I held my breath and listened for breathing. I couldn't hear any. I slowly opened my eyes and looked around. Laude was lying next to me, eyes open, head still down. Her head picked up when she saw me moving. It was just the two of us.

"How's my good girl today?" Her ears perked up and her tail started to wag.

I looked at my aching right arm. The bandage was intact but bloodied. I started to get out of bed and was startled to hear Craig on the other side of the door. "Are you ok? I called out of work today. I figured I'd need to re-do your bandage." It would be thoughtful if he hadn't been the cause of the gash.

"Thanks."

He unlocked the door and came in. "I'll be right with you, Laude." Craig patted her on the head and came over to me. I was standing on the far side of the bed.

"I think I can re-do the bandage if you leave the supplies. I'd rather take a shower first."

He took my hand and looked closer at the bandage. "Ok. I'll just take Laude out." He kept a firm grip on my hand. He was done looking at the bandage but wasn't done with me.

He took a deep breath and quietly asked, "Could we try again on our anniversary?"

"Sure."

"I'll pick you up tonight."

Craig knocked on the door for our make-up date, earlier tonight because he didn't go to work. I hadn't even heard him leave the house all day.

I had decided I'd be on good behavior tonight. Besides running out of options, I was tired. My desperate antics the night before somehow didn't push Craig over the edge. I felt it best to be well behaved. I told Laude the plan before we left. She just looked up at me and wagged her tail. She was always on good behavior.

He was pleased to see me in the first outfit he had given me, the red dress. My legs wobbled in the heels, sore from the jump out the window and the fall when he caught me.

"You look beautiful, Aud..," he cleared his throat. "Lillian! Beautiful, Lillian. Tonight is going to be a better night!"

We filed up the stairs, me, Laude, followed by Craig. I hesitated at the top of the stairs. I figured with the window being broken we would eat in the kitchen. I was wrong. He escorted us into the dining room. The window was fixed and there was an alarm system at the front door.

I sat in my chair and he placed a harness over me. It crossed over my chest and buckled in the back. Another new addition to his home.

Before I could ask about it, he said, while grinning, "So you don't run away, again."

I was angry. My good girl routine didn't last five minutes. "Seriously, this is ridiculous." Struggling, I tried to reach the buckle but couldn't. He just watched me, grinning. "Do you really think this is necessary?," I asked.

"As I said, I just don't want you running again," he answered, still grinning.

"So, you don't think I can run with this?" I gestured up and down at the chair.

"Well, I was hoping for a quiet evening. But that would certainly liven it up." He looked away, considering the idea. "Yes, I would like to see you try that."

A normal woman would have admitted he had called her bluff. I accepted the challenge. I got up and ran. We both knew I wouldn't get far. It wasn't a true escape attempt. It was the principle. I made it five feet before I fell. It was harder than I imagined. The chair limited my stride length and my posture.

I landed on my left side and heard something break. Not feeling any pain, I knew it was the chair leg and not my own. As I pictured how I must have looked, I couldn't suppress my laughter. Craig knelt down beside me, laughing too. Laude was licking my face and that made us laugh even harder.

Still on my side, tears rolling down my face, I said, "I told you I could do it."

"And, I told you it would liven up the evening."

I wasn't sure how long we stayed in that position- me on my side, broken chair attached to me, laughing; Laude circling us barking; Craig laughing by my side. Eventually the laughter subsided and Laude exhausted or maybe dizzy, stopped her running.

Craig reached over me and detached the harness. I had been this close to him before but had never noticed how good he smelled. I couldn't identify it but it smelled clean, fresh. I remembered when Annie and I had gone cologne shopping for Jeffrey. The salesperson told us all about the colognes, the different "notes". I didn't like any of them. They were over-powering.

Craig didn't smell like he had cologne on. I heard the buckle snap open and I wiggled out of it. Craig held out his hand, which I accepted. He helped me up with a little more force than was necessary and I fell into his chest. I looked up at him and our eyes locked.

We stood for several moments that way and he started to lean in to kiss me.

Our lips less than an inch apart, Laude snapped me out of it by barking. I couldn't say good girl but I thought it. I turned away and shook my head. The remnants of the chair caught my eye.

I turned back to him and said, "Sorry about the chair."

"Totally worth it," he grinned. I looked up into his face.

I don't know if it was the absurdity of the moment or Stockholm syndrome, but I saw a man I liked.

LILY

Friday   March 27, 2009

Three dates in three nights. It was a personal record for me.

The atmosphere was different when he escorted me upstairs. At the top of the stairs, Craig told me to go into the living room, while he got some drinks. He had never directed me into a room before and left before seeing I was where I was supposed to be. Classical music played lightly.

When he came back in carrying two champagne glasses and a champagne bottle in an ice bucket, he found me looking at the front door. I wondered what the alarm code was. He seemed sappy enough to use my birthday and that would be my first guess. I wasn't planning to use it but just curious what number he'd pick.

"They say third times the charm. This has been chilled since the 25th!"

Laude jumped at the uncorking of the bottle and I soothed her by stroking her back. Craig poured the champagne carefully into the glasses. The bubbles quickly rose to the top but stopped before running over.

I remembered New Year's Eve with my parents when I was a kid. Dad would open the bottle and champagne always spilled out. More would bubble over when he poured it into the glasses. Mom teased him that she was lucky to get a glassful by the time he was finished. She'd always give me a little sip. It was the only time I had ever had champagne.

Craig handed me a glass. "To my Christmas wish come true." We clinked glasses. I tried not to think about that wish. Christmas had been a difficult day. It was the first without my parents; without my aunt; without anyone. I left the house only to walk Laude. The longest time I'd been out was that evening, when we sat on one of the boardwalk's benches. Crying.

I took a sip. It was good and sweet. I had never liked it when my mom had given it to me; maybe because this was pink. I finished my glass and placed it on the coffee table.

This time the bubbles really did go to my head. I rarely drank and alcohol's immediate effects were that I would say what I was thinking. Rarely a good thing.

Before I knew it, I heard myself say "Craig, where is this going?" Such a girl.

"What do you mean?"

"I mean, what's your end game? What's the plan?"

"I'm not sure what you mean? Do you mean tonight or in general?"

"Yes, I mean in general. Where do you think we'll be in one year? Will I still be here?"

"I hope so."

"Do you hope or is that your plan?"

"Of course, that's my plan. But I didn't plan to tell you three months in that I see us together forever. That I see myself marrying you."

"I'd have to be able to get out of this house to do that." He looked bewildered.

My brain was telling me to stop but the champagne kept pushing me. "What are you waiting for?"

"What do you mean what am I waiting for? We've been together three months. I thought you'd need a little more time." He answered, still confused.

"Together three months! You mean *you've* had a relationship with me for three months. Six weeks of this *relationship* I wasn't a knowing participant. I'm still not a willing participant." He sat there stunned.

"Did you ever think of coming up to me that night? Did you ever think about coming up to me while I sat on that bench alone, crying and ask me what was wrong? Or trying to be nice?"

"No." He hesitated. "Yes, yes, I did. That's what I wanted. To go over to you, get you to stop crying, make you feel better. I told you I hate to see you cry. But I thought you'd think it was weird. That you'd get creeped out with some stranger coming up to you at night on the deserted boardwalk."

I remembered how I had wished someone had been there with me that night, other than Laude. Someone to talk to about the great Christmas memories I had- midnight mass, presents, carols, dinner, my family. I had debated calling Annie, but didn't want to spoil Harry's first Christmas. I wanted to talk to Aunt Florence; but she didn't talk to me anyone. I had wished for someone, so I wouldn't be alone. Craig was my Christmas wish that didn't go as plan.

"Yes, this is a far less weird way to go about meeting me." My volume went up as I gestured around at the room. "Stalking me. Watching me in my apartment! Rigging an online dating site once you learned I was on it. What are you going to do next? What are you waiting for?"

When we had first sat down, Laude was at my feet. She now snuggled in between my legs. I could feel her starting to shake. She hated loud voices.

"You know what I'm waiting for. I'm waiting for you to look at me the way you look at that door." He hesitated, then added, "with longing."

Sometimes when I caught Craig looking at me I wasn't sure what he was thinking. I never saw lust in his eyes. I never feared he was going to attack me and rape me. What I saw was just that, longing. He longed for me to return his love.

"And what is so great about your life that you want so badly to return to it? You don't go out. You don't like your job. I saw you crying so many nights. *I hate to see you cry*. You don't have any friends in the area. For God's sake, you were alone on Christmas!" His volume matched my own. "No one has even noticed you are gone!"

Tears started pooling in my eyes. He got up and started pacing behind the couch he had been sitting on.

Before he could go on about the shortcomings of my old life, I shouted louder than I had ever shouted before, *"I'm in mourning. I'm adjusting to my parents' deaths."* I wiped the tears away as he stood behind the couch, stunned. He was horrified. It was obvious he had no idea about my parent's death.

He started to walk over to me.

"NO! Stop! Don't come near me. Don't touch me." I got up from the couch, trying to keep distance between us. I walked backwards, away from him. Sobbing, screaming at him to stay away, I walked into the wall and then into the corner of the room. I slid down and curled into a ball. "Just go away!"

This was why I hadn't gone on any dates since their death. Even Annie had never seen one of these meltdowns. I certainly didn't want a new man to. It would be a surefire relationship killer.

I don't know how long I stayed like that. I eventually calmed down and wondered how much worse I had made everything. Did I kill this particular relationship? And what would that mean for Laude and I? I opened my eyes to find Laude sitting by my feet, her normal position when I cried. I expected to find Craig there. I had never heard him leave.

After a few minutes of quiet, Craig came back in with a cup of tea and a box of tissues. He placed them near me.

His eyes were red. Not with rage as I had expected, but as if he had been crying too.

I wondered- what would have happened if he had sat next to me on that bench Christmas night?

I drank the tea in silence, still sitting in the corner. He sat on the couch he had been on. He could see me but he wasn't watching me.

I finished the tea. I stood up and walked over to him. We were almost eye to eye. "I'm sorry for that outburst." I was. "It's been several months but their death was a shock and I'm still adjusting. I wish you hadn't seen that." Again, the truth.

"It's nothing to be sorry for. I'm sorry I didn't know. I should have known. I heard you say once you were grieving. I saw the books on grief in your home. I thought it was your aunt. I wouldn't have pushed."

He stood up and towered over me. "We have more in common than you think. The sudden, unexpected death of two loved ones is difficult. It can be too much to bear and can lead you to do desperate things." Our bodies stood inches apart. He leaned over and kissed the top of my head. He took my hand and led Laude and I back to our room. I crawled on the bed, lying on my right side, despite my bandaged arm smarting.

Laude barked at him as he said good night. "Good night to you too, Laude." I heard her run up the stairs. "Sorry, I forgot to take her out. I'll be right back."

I heard him go up the stairs but I didn't hear either door close or lock. I rolled over and was surprised to see the bedroom door wide open. I told myself that I didn't get up and try to run because he had Laude, because I knew he'd catch me yet again. Truth was he had asked a good question. Why was I so eager to get back to a life I didn't like? A life where no one missed me?

Craig was right about one other thing too. Third time was a charm.

LILY

Saturday   March 28, 2009

I enjoyed far more freedom after that night. I told myself I was working my newest plan. He said he wanted to see longing in my eyes and he was going to get it. Sadly, I didn't think he would see anything disingenuous. It was more genuine than I wanted to admit to myself or to anyone else.

I woke to Laude jumping off the bed when she heard Craig come down the stairs. I reached for the remote to put on the local news as I did every morning, in hopes of seeing myself; of seeing Annie pleading for my safe return, a call for any information, a promise of a reward for 'Franklin's' arrest. Craig's words last night rang in my ears. "No one has even noticed you are gone."

I stared at the television, still off and left it that way.

I had heard Craig come down as usual to get Laude for her walk but realized I hadn't heard the dog door latch click open. I rolled over to see the bedroom door open. Craig had opened the door, not the doggie door, to let her out and left it open. I wasn't sure if it was a peace offering or an invitation. I got out of bed and marveled as I walked through the open door. I slowly walked up the stairs, calling out to Craig a few times without response.

I peaked into the living room and wondered who the loved ones he lost were. I had always thought his home had been decorated by a woman. One had to be his wife. The home wasn't childproofed, so I didn't think the second was a child. I stepped back into the foyer and looked up the stairs to the second level. I wondered if I'd find a nursery up there but I doubted it.

I smelled fresh coffee brewing. I imagined the white smoke beckoning me into the kitchen. I stared at the brewing pot of coffee. It had been weeks, no months, since I had a cup of coffee. I cringed when I remembered the last time I had a cup of coffee was with 'Franklin', on our date. I shook the image out of my head and took a deep breath of the delicious aroma. When Craig and Laude came back in, they found me staring at the machine as it completed brewing.

"Oh good. You're up."

I knelt and scratched Laude behind her ears. "Were you a good girl, Laude?"

"Of course she was!," he answered, smiling at both of us.

She lost interest with me as she heard Craig rustling with a bag in the pantry. He poured her food into a bowl and placed it on the floor.

"I think the coffee is ready. I'd ask if you want some but I don't need to." He took two mugs out of a cabinet and poured coffee into them. He filled his to the top and left mine with enough room for plenty of milk. Why hadn't I noticed on my date with Franklin that he had fixed my coffee the way I liked it without asking?

"What do you want from the bakery tomorrow?," he asked.

A completely abnormal situation was slowly becoming my new normal.

NATHAN

Monday   March 29, 2009

It had been over a week since I had talked to Annie. She had left two messages. It was hard to call her when I had nothing to report. I thought it was even worse to call her and not tell her what I had found out. She would go berserk if I told her about Charlie driving the Brannon's off the road. There was nothing I could do with that information but keep it to myself. I wondered if I would tell Lily, if I ever found her.

I called Annie, hoping to get voicemail. She answered on the first ring.

"Nathan, how are you? You must have been busy."

"I'm sorry I haven't called sooner. But..."

"But, you have nothing to report and you're sorry you ever agreed to look into this." She cleared her throat. "You think she left like the other cops. Every time I call them, they say there's no evidence of foul play. There's nothing to look into. I called the local media. They don't care either. I can't tell you how many people I called. I couldn't find one station, one reporter who would look into it!" I heard a male voice in the background and then her muffled voice, "I am not yelling at him." She returned to speaking to me, "I'm sorry, Nathan. I'm frustrated and I know you want to quit."

"No, no, Annie. That's not it at all." Quitting was not an option. I needed to find Lily. "I know she's been taken but I don't know by whom, where, how, or why." I rethought the statement. "Basically,

Annie, I've spent a month and have found nothing. She's been gone six weeks." The silence lingered. "I don't know else what to do."

"But you're not giving up?," she asked.

"Not until we find her." I heard her sigh. "Or until you kick me out of her place," I laughed. It wasn't so funny when I realized I probably wouldn't even stop then.

NATHAN

Wednesday   4:30 a.m.   April 1, 2009

I woke up to a sharp beep. I was initially disoriented. I had slept at Lily's again; in Lily's bed, again. The beep sounded once more. I looked up at the smoke alarm. I didn't remember seeing any spare batteries anywhere in her home. I cringed at the thought of listening to the beeping for the few more hours of sleep I could have. I got up and walked over to the alarm as it sounded again. I reached up and twisted it back and forth until it unhinged. I couldn't see the battery and turned on the light. I squinted as my eyes adjusted to the bright light.

As I re-opened my eyes fully, the first thing I noticed was not the battery but a camera. I shook my head and rubbed my eyes. I couldn't imagine that I was really seeing a surveillance camera. I looked closer as it beeped again. I went out to the dining room and grabbed a chair. I brought it into the bedroom for a closer look. I detached the battery and the beeping stopped. I stood, stunned, that a security camera was in Lily's bedroom. I went into the living room and looked at the other smoke detector. It was the same model as the one in the bedroom. I unhinged it and found a camera as well.

I took out the memory card. It looked like the one I used for my digital camera. I had no way to view the images here. I wondered how long this had been here.

And I wondered what else Tony did when he was helping Lily with things around the apartment.

I was waiting outside Tony's office when he came off the elevator. He smiled when he saw me. "How you doing?," he asked.

"What is this?" I held out the smoke detector, wrapped in a paper towel.

"Looks like a smoke detector."

"Look a little closer." I handed it to him. "Don't touch it," I snapped.

He looked at it carefully and handed it back, still wrapped in the paper towel. "I don't know what it is. It must be one of those nanny cams. I've never seen one of these." He walked past me and started to unlock his office.

"It was in Lily's bedroom and living room."

He turned around shocked. Shaking his head, "I don't know how it got there."

"You're the only one that *'helped'* her with things," I reminded him.

His voice raised in volume and pitch. "I never helped her with this. This wasn't in her apartment in October. I changed the batteries when the clocks changed. She must have put up some new ones."

"A girl who *you* said couldn't do anything in her home put up a security camera, to watch herself?"

"I know what you're trying to say. But I didn't put it up there. I've been nice to you but I think its time for you to go." He entered his office and threw his bag on the floor. There was no room on either desk for it. The office was even more disarrayed than the last time I'd been in it. He sat down, holding his head in his hands, pulling on his remaining hair.

"I'm taking this to the precinct. If I find your prints on it, I'll be back."

I drove over to the Long Beach police department, thankful I had the day off. I started to go in and then decided I'd better call first.

Departments could get touchy about other police officers bringing in evidence.

I called Steve on his cell. "Steve, I found something in Lily's apartment. You working?"

"Are you kidding? You still in that girl's apartment? How long has it been? Girls gone, bud."

"Lay off Steve. I found a surveillance camera."

"Maybe she was spying on the dog walker."

"In her bedroom?"

"Maybe she thought she was stealing from her."

"You working or not? Can I bring it by? I can't take this in to New York."

"You're going to bring it if I say yes or no, aren't you?"

"Yes."

"You're outside, aren't you?"

"Yes."

"You owe me a beer."

And he hung up. I'd owe him a case if he got me a lead.

Steve was at his desk, drinking coffee. He looked at his watch. "Parking lot must be full. It took you a whole minute to get in here."

I handed him the smoke detector/surveillance camera in a ziploc bag. I should have put it in there originally. My supervisors would have reamed me if they had known how I had originally handled the evidence.

"I've touched it but no one else has. I showed it to the super who denied ever seeing it.

I believe him."

He placed it on his desk. "Ok, I'll take it for prints."

I took the memory card out of my pocket. "I have this. Can we watch it here?"

He paused and looked at the card. "What were you thinking touching it?"

"It was the middle of the night. I wasn't thinking. I had just wanted the beeping to stop."

"What the hell? Are you living there?"

"No, I'm not living there. Sometimes I stay there. I keep hoping something will click. And look it did!"

He glared at me.

"This is your case. We can watch it here." I didn't want to drive home to watch it on my computer. I didn't think Steve would let me leave with it anyway.

"There is no case, Nathan."

"But there is a surveillance camera. If Lily had put up a surveillance camera, she would have told Annie. Plus, I don't think Lily could have put up one of these. The super did everything for her."

"Do you hear yourself? You're talking about people you don't even know as if you've known them forever." He snatched the memory card from my hand and put it in his computer.

I pulled up a chair next to him. We watched in silence as the video started. It was better quality video than the building had in the lobby. It showed a steady stream of video when motion was detected and for about two minutes after motion had stopped. Unfortunately, all we saw was me-watching TV on the couch, eating dinner, drinking a Sam Adams- the beer Lily liked- on the couch, and on Lily's computer. Ten minutes into the video, I looked to see Steve staring at me, shocked. I reached across him and fast forwarded through the rest of the video. I was the only one on this card.

I took the other memory card out of my pocket. "Maybe this one will be better?" I didn't turn to look at him.

"Will we see more of you? Over the past several weeks? Living in someone else's apartment?"

I hesitated, not wanting to admit it. "Probably. But let's look anyway."

"You better hope you don't find this girl. She's gonna be pretty pissed to come home and find 'Papa Bear' sleeping in her bed!" He snatched the card from my hand and put it in the computer.

I had had the same thought myself once when I woke up in the middle of the night in her bed. What would she do if she came home and found a stranger in her apartment, never mind in her bed? My luck, Steve would be the arresting officer. He'd love every minute of it. Hopefully, Annie would bail me out.

I drove back to Lily's. I was disappointed by another dead end. The surveillance videos had not shown anything but me. The smoke detector had no fingerprints but my own.

I debated calling Annie to fill her in.

But why get her hopes up for nothing? All I could tell her was that someone had been watching Lily prior to her disappearance.

I hadn't told her about my second meeting with Charlie and Florence. When she had called me that week, I had diverted the conversation onto Harry. I don't know why I hadn't told her. At least she would have known I wasn't wasting time. But I felt Lily should know first. She should do with that information whatever she wanted, including tell Annie if she wanted. I still believed I would find her. I had no reason to believe it but I did.

I called anyway. It went to voicemail after the fourth ring and I debated hanging up. Instead, I left a brief message asking her to call me when she could. Before I hung up, Annie's number flashed on the screen. I took a deep breath and clicked 'accept'.

"Nathan, Nathan. You there?" I could hear her gasping for breath and Harry crying in the background. She must have run for the phone.

"Yes, I'm here, Annie."

"You learn anything new?"

"Yes, but it's not as helpful as I had hoped."

"What happened?"

"I found a surveillance camera in her apartment. Two actually."

"What?"

"The smoke detectors in her bedroom and living room had cameras in them. I'm assuming she didn't put them up."

"No. Oh my god. Are you saying Tony has been spying on her? Do you think he hurt her?"

"I thought that too. But, after talking to him, I don't think so. He seemed truly surprised to see it."

"You're right. I can't imagine Tony doing that. I only met him once or twice. He seemed like a nice old man."

"Who else would have access to her apartment?"

"No one I can think of. Except the dog walker."

"She changed the locks after moving in, right?"

"Yes, I was there when Tony did it. I told her to. Got the new lock for her, too." She spoke to Harry a few words and he finally quieted down. Eagerly, she asked, "You took it to the police right? What do they think?"

"They think she left, Annie."

"But you don't do you?"

"No."

NATHAN

6 p.m.   Sunday   April 5, 2009

I rode up to the fifth floor with Ms. June. "You sure are here a lot," she said as the doors closed. Not the first person to say that to me this week. "You learning anything?," she asked.

I hesitated because I didn't want to admit it, to myself or to anyone else. "No."

"I sure hope you're better at your real job than at this job of finding Genevieve." I hoped so, too. I also hoped Ms. June didn't see me cringe at the insult.

"It's too bad. I sure miss that dog. Everyone asks me about her."

I didn't bother to ask if anyone asked about Lillian. I knew no one did. We stared as the numbers slowly ticked up to five.

I held my arm across the door. "You first, Ms. June."

"Thank you, Nathan."

We walked in silence down the corridor to our respective apartments. I corrected myself; this was not my apartment. Ms. June was right that I was spending a lot of time here. Too much time if you asked Steve. If anyone else knew, they would agree. I wondered what Annie would think if she knew how often I stayed here. I didn't think she'd mind as long as I found Lily.

I fumbled in my pocket for the keys and dropped my folder on Lily. The folder that I carried everywhere in the hopes I would learn something new by scrolling through my notes for the ump-teenth time.

"Shit." Ms. June turned around. Embarrassed, I look up at her and said, "Sorry, ma'am."

"No problem. I've heard worse, young man."

She started to reach for the papers that were splayed on the floor. "Don't worry. I can get it," I said, trying to prevent her from leaning over and possibly falling. I held my breath as she ignored me and picked up the papers closest to her. She looked at them and tried to get them in order. She stopped at one and looked up at me.

"Why do you have a picture of Franco?" As I stared at her, she continued, "Tony's assistant, Franco. You looking for him, too?"

"What?" I couldn't have heard her right.

She held up the 'Journey to Love' picture of Franklin. "This is Franco without the glasses and beard."

I stared at her in shock. I had shown the picture to Tony and he hadn't recognized him. I had shown the picture at Roaster's several times and no one had recognized him.

"Now that I think about it, they both went missing about the same time. Tony said he was sick. But then Franco just stopped calling. Tony said his phone's disconnected now."

"Could you come in for a little bit, Ms. June?"

"If you think it would help." I opened the door. She went in and sat at the dining room table. I flopped down in the chair across from her.

Ms. June looked up from the photo. "So, you're looking for Franco too?"

"Well, now I am," I mumbled.

"What do you mean 'now I am'?"

I closed my eyes, wishing she hadn't heard me, surprised her hearing was that good. "I didn't really think the man in the photo had anything to do with Lillian's disappearance. I didn't know Tony's assistant, Franco, never returned."

She held out the photo, accusingly. "Why didn't you show this to me earlier?"

"I showed it to Tony and he didn't recognize him." I shook my head. "The staff at Roaster's didn't recognize him either and according to Tony, Franco went there every workday."

"Who did you think it is if you didn't know it was Franco?"

"He's Franklin. Or who I thought was Franklin. Lillian's friend set her up on a date with him from a website."

"Damn dating sites. I met my husband at a dance during the war."

"What do you remember about Franco?"

"He was in this apartment a lot when he first started. Tony was in here a lot too so I didn't think much of it. I figured Tony got tired of fixing things for her so he delegated it the new guy. Figured he wouldn't share the money with Franco either. I caught him twice coming out of here in two days. He looked real nervous. But, I figured it was because he was new."

It was all fitting into place. The smoke detector surveillance camera. He was coming in to check it.

I put my head down. I had known since early on it had to be someone with access to the building. How did I miss seeing Franco on the lobby's surveillance camera?

NATHAN

Monday   9 a.m.   April 6, 2009

"Hey, Tony. Sorry about last time," I told him as he got off the elevator. I handed him a large coffee. I had been waiting by his door for the last ten minutes.

"You should be sorry. Thinking that I would spy on Lillian. That I'd spy on anyone. That kind of talk could get me fired." I followed him into the office and sat down as he did.

"I know. I'm sorry. I never said it to anyone else." He took a large sip of the coffee.   "This is still good. Thanks." I thought I would have to grovel for forgiveness a little more but the coffee seemed to please Tony enough.

"I found out who put in the cameras."

"Really. Who?" He leaned back in his chair and took another sip.

"Franco."

He leaned forward quickly and coughed on his last sip. After clearing his throat, "What?"

"It was Franco. I don't know if he got a job here because he was stalking Lillian or if he started stalking Lillian after getting the job."

He shook his head. "Nope. No way. He was a good worker. I never noticed anything."

"Ms. June identified his picture."

"What picture?"

"The one I showed you before I watched the surveillance tapes."

"That wasn't Franco. I told you I didn't know the man in that picture."

"Ms. June was positive it was Franco, without the beard and glasses." I showed him the picture again. He looked at it intently and shook his head.

"Oh, no. Maybe she's right. I don't know." He continued studying the picture. "I really don't know," and handed it back to me. "He asked about Lillian once. Asked me why she was so sad. I told him I thought her Aunt Florence had died. You know, I had thought they'd make a nice couple. They were both so nice but shy. He was so good here. Such a hard worker." He shook his head. "I really can't believe this."

My blood boiled at the thought of Lily with someone else. "Can I have his information?," I asked.

Tony hesitated, started to get up, then sat back down. "You sure? I just don't think it could have been him."

"I'm sure. I just hope there's something in his personnel file that might help me."

"Personnel file? I have a copy of his driver's license and resume." He got up and walked over to the file cabinet. He flipped through a few files then picked out a thin file.

"Here you go."

I opened it and scanned the documents.

"No criminal record report? No background check?"

Tony looked up guiltily. "No. I interviewed him. I was desperate for help. He was the only one who applied."

"How did you meet him?"

"He just walked in one day and asked if we were hiring. I hired him on the spot."

"References?"

"I called his references. They all had good things to say."

"Do you have the references?"

"It's on the back of the resume." I flipped over the resume to find three names and numbers.

"How did you pay him?"

"The managing agent paid him. By check."

"Do you have any of the cashed checks back?"

"You'll have to talk to Ronnie. The board would be able to get that information for you."

Tony gave me Ronnie's number. I called and left a message.

I went to work early to check the department of motor vehicles website. I was disappointed but not surprised to learn there was no "Franco Cradic" ever to have a New York driver's license.

My cell rang. "Miccoli," I answered.

"This is Ronnie, returning your call. You wanted to talk to me about Lillian again?" I had talked to him briefly when I first took the case. He didn't know Lillian. He had seen her a few times at board meetings with Florence but had never spoken to her.

"Yes, I think Franco, the superintendent's assistant, had something to do with her disappearance."

"Why do you think that?" He sounded doubtful.

"'Franco Cradic' is an alias."

"How do you know that?"

"His driver's license is fake. Just checked."

"Oh."

"I wanted to know what bank he cashed his checks at."

"I have to call the building's accountant for that. It might take a day or so."

"Please get it as fast as possible. The faster I find this Franco, the faster I find Lillian."

Five minutes passed and my cell rang again. Ronnie said, "This is strange. It doesn't look like Franco ever cashed any of the checks. Can you imagine working for weeks and not cashing the checks?"

I could. He wasn't working for money but for information. And he got plenty.

LILY

April 6, 2009

I was reading a book, while lying on the couch. Craig was on the opposite sofa, reading the paper. Now, whenever Craig was on the first floor, he left the bedroom door unlocked. I didn't always go upstairs but if Laude didn't return from her walks I'd go up to look for her. I think he gave her snacks to keep her with him, knowing I'd soon follow.

He grabbed his glass and got up stiffly.

"Is your back ok?," I asked.

"Oh, it's nothing," he answered, while rubbing his back. "I forget you're a physical therapist sometimes. Never saw you at work."

So the extent of his stalking was Long Beach. Although I shouldn't be, I was always surprised when he'd reveal a little more about what he knew about me and how he knew it.

"I sit too much at my new job. I miss moving around," he added.

"Your last job didn't have you at a desk all day? I thought that's all a computer programmer would do." I shrugged and went back to the book.

"My last job was very active. Sometimes I didn't get my day's run in." Craig told me he ran everyday, three to five miles, averaging a six minute mile. It was no wonder I had never out run him.

"Sometimes, I'd come home and after doing a few things around the house," he winked at me then continued, "I'd just pass out on the couch." 'A few things' obviously meaning building and decorating my prison, probably watching his daily video feed of me. Yes, I'm sure that kept him busy.

He rattled on about his old job more and I tuned out, only able to visualize his post work activities of stalking me. I heard him say a name and realized it was the first time he had every used someone's name. He would tell stories about 'a friend' or a 'co-worker', but he never said their name. I heard him say 'Tony' again. "Tony used to give me all the tough jobs. All the heavy lifting. I would curse him then but I miss it now. Those six weeks working at the condo really built me up."

He said 'Tony' as if I knew him. I held my breath and tried not to react as I realized who Tony was. The only Tony I knew was the superintendent at the condo. Working with Tony would have given Craig full access to my apartment, during the many hours I was at work. It was how he installed a carbon monoxide detector, put up two smoke detectors with surveillance cameras, knew what size clothes I wore, what foods I ate and taught Laude how to shake hands. Without me ever seeing him.

"You, ok? You've been staring at the same page for the past five minutes."

NATHAN

Tuesday   7 p.m.   April 7, 2009

I waited a day to call Annie.
"You don't sound good. You alright?," she asked.
"Not really. I have some good news and some bad news."
"How bad?" She was sniffling, holding back tears.
I heard Jeffrey in the background. "Annie, what's wrong?"
"Not that bad, Annie. I'm sorry. I haven't found her."
"What did you learn?"
"I know who took her."
"That's great! Nathan, that's a huge break." She covered the phone. "It's ok. He knows who took her. He's going to find her, Jeffrey."
"Annie, I don't know where he is."
"But you'll find him. You're going to find her!" She was so excited. She wasn't going to sound so excited when she learned who it was.
"How'd you do it? Who is he? How can I help?" She spit the questions out. I didn't know what to answer first. "Nathan, who is it?"
"It was Franco, Tony's assistant."
"I didn't know Tony had an assistant."
"He was new. I'm not sure if he got the job and then started to stalk Lily or the other way around."
"I don't think Lily ever met him."
"She probably didn't. She would have told you. She definitely would have told you after the date."

"Date? What date?," she asked.

"The date you set her up on." I heard a quick intake of breath on her side of the line. The silence felt like it lasted hours.

I broke the silence. "Franco is Franklin."

No matter what I said, she would feel guilty. "This was a well devised plan. If he hadn't met her on the website, he would have found another way." I heard a thump and Annie wailing.

Jeffrey got on the phone. "What's going on? What did you tell her?"

Annie was sobbing in the background. "It's my fault," she cried out in between sobs.

"I know who took Lily," I told him.

"*I know that.* She told me that. But why is she so upset about it?"

"It was Franklin, from that dating site."

"Oh no." He hung up as Annie's sobs grew louder and Harry joined in.

I made another call I had put off making. I figured I should get it out of the way.

"Hey, Nathan."

"Hey, Steve. You said I owed you a drink."

"You probably owe me a few."

"Meet at Sammie's in ten minutes?"

"Sure. Katie's at the gym."

I hung up before he could question how I could be there so fast.

As I parked, I saw Steve walking up the block. "Guess you're still staying at *Lily's*."

"Good guess." I wasn't in the mood for him. I walked past him and straight to the bar. "Two Sam Adams."

As the bartender walked away, Steve sat down on the stool next to me. "Sam Adams? When you start drinking that? We always have Corona."

"Fine." I waved my hand to get the bartender to change the order.

Sensing my annoyance, Steve grabbed me arm. "No, it's ok. I'll try it."

I pulled my arm away. "Sorry, it's me. Tough day."

I drank half of the beer before Steve had even taken a sip of his. Steve was watching me, debating what to say. "I'm guessing you are no closer to finding her."

"No." I sighed, shaking my head. "Each time I get a break it leads nowhere!" I finished the beer and ordered another. "Charlie kills her parents. He doesn't know he did it. Florence covers it up. She has an alibi. Franco sets up the cameras. But it's an alias. And a good one. His references were one of those damn companies that supplies fake references! He never cashed his checks. The address on his resume is fake. Cell phone disconnected. I have nothing to go on."

"What are you talking about?," he asked as I started my second beer. "Oh my god. You're talking about Lily. You found all that out. You're serious. You actually found out who took her." Talking more to himself than to me, he continued, "Someone actually took her."

I had forgotten he was there. My rant had really been for myself.

"*Yes, someone took her! I've been telling you that for weeks!*" I yelled as I banged my fist on the bar. The other patrons looked at me. Steve waved them off.

"I...I just can't believe it. I really just thought she left." We finished our beers in silence.

He placed his empty bottle down and turned to me, "How can I help?"

We went back to Lily's and went through the large file I had amassed over the past six weeks. Steve couldn't believe the volume of information I had collected.

"Little good it did me. I'm still no closer to finding her."

"But you know the who and why. We'll find her."

LILY

Wednesday   April 8, 2009

I woke up to Laude's moaning. It was two in the morning and I was disoriented. "Laude?"

I looked around but couldn't see her. I turned on the bedside lamp and squinted from its brightness. Laude wasn't on the bed.

I got up and found her by her doggie door. She was curled up and whimpering. I petted her and asked "What's wrong, Laude?" She didn't even lift her head. I looked around the room and saw she had vomited. There was something red in it and I panicked.

I banged on the walls and started screaming for Craig. Laude didn't investigate all the noise. She remained curled up by the door. "Craig, Craig, please come downstairs!" I continued banging on the walls, "Please Craig! Laude's sick! I don't know what to do!"

It seemed like forever before I heard noise upstairs. The bedside clock said I had been up five minutes. I ran back over to Laude who hadn't moved. She just whimpered.

I heard Craig running down the stairs to our room. I feared he'd rush in and run over both of us. "I'm by the door with Laude. Don't run in."

He opened the door slowly, dressed only in blue striped boxer shorts. He knelt down next to us. "What's wrong?"

"I don't know. I woke up to her moaning. She threw up over there. I think there's blood in it."

"OK, baby. Let's go out." He gently picked her up. I followed them up the stairs and out the back door.

"Do you have to potty, Laude?" He put her down and she slowly walked away from us. She circled a few times before hunching her back to go the bathroom. Laude had diarrhea.

"She followed me in the kitchen yesterday and I gave her something I shouldn't have. A piece of tomato. It didn't say anything in the dog book about not giving a dog a tomato. Before you moved in, I wanted to make sure I knew everything I could about taking care of Laude. She likes pizza so I thought it'd be alright." He turned to me, "I'm sorry. Maybe that's what made her sick."

"It's o.k. She's walking now. I think she'll be fine." I didn't remember him taking my right hand but I felt him shivering. He gently rubbed his thumb against my ring finger. "Go in. You're cold. I'll watch her."

"Let me get us some jackets." He turned and returned to the house. I watched Laude. She walked a few feet and got sick again.

Looking back I realized I could have run then. The idea never entered my mind.

Craig returned a few minutes later with two jackets and two pairs of shoes. He didn't look surprised to see me standing in the same spot. The thought of me trying to escape hadn't entered his mind either.

I hadn't noticed how cold my feet were until I put on his slippers. He helped me into his jacket and then put one on himself. We sat on the stoop and watched Laude for a few more minutes before she came to us. Her tail was wagging slowly. Her ears were perked up.

"She looks better." Craig patted her on her head. "Let's get you some water, little girl." He picked her up and I followed them back into the house, to the kitchen. He put her down after filling her water dish with fresh water. She lapped it up while we stood over her watching.

"She looks fine now." We both said at the same time and then laughed.

She looked up at us at the sound of our laughter.

Craig walked over to the coffee pot and brought it to the sink to fill it. "Sit down. I'll make us some coffee."

"It's two in the morning, Craig. We'll never get back to sleep."

"I thought we should stay up to watch her."

She ran over to me. I got on the floor with her and rubbed her back.

"I think she's fine. But I am cold. Do you have hot cocoa?"

"Sure. You're right. She looks alright."

We watched Laude's every move while drinking the hot cocoa. She was tired and had settled at my feet. When we were finished, I picked Laude up and headed downstairs. I stopped at the doorway and said "Thank you," as he washed the mugs.

He replied "You're welcome" and we returned to our respective bedrooms.

NATHAN

Wednesday   April 8, 2009

Steve and I had spent hours going through everything again, and again. The chief still didn't believe it was a missing person's case. He refused to put a detective on it. We were looking for her without any other resources. Chief Sonja listened to us for five minutes and then kicked us out of his office. He kicked me out of the precinct when I continued arguing. Steve restrained me from making the situation worse.

Steve was able to use department resources to find out a few things I couldn't. Franco/Franklin's cell phone was a burn phone; untraceable. His 'Journey to Love' account had been paid by an untraceable gift card.

We spoke to everyone in the building on our day off. Few recognized Franco from the photographs. We had the one Annie had from the dating website and we made one with Ms. June's help, adding a beard and glasses. Few could remember Tony having an assistant at all. No one remembered ever talking to him. Despite continued questioning, Tony could not remember anything personal about Franco. He couldn't remember what car he drove. He wasn't even sure if he did drive to work.

Steve and I ended the day, sitting on Lily's patio, drinking beers, Sam Adams. I had stocked Lily's fridge with the beer Annie said Lily liked.

As the sun set, he said "I'm sorry, Nathan." I wasn't sure what he was sorry for - that he never believed me that she was missing, that he never tried to look for her, that the chief refused to believe us, that we accomplished nothing today or that neither of us knew what to do next. It didn't matter.

"So am I, Steve."

LILY

Monday   April 13, 2009

Normally, I wouldn't watch the Mets pre-game show on Opening Day. Normally I'd be there. I hadn't bought tickets this year, though. I said it was on principle. Opening Day should be a day game, not a 7:10pm start. That's what I had told myself. It was easier than admitting I had no one to go with. "The Saturday-ers" sat together for the thirteen Saturday home games each year, but never on Opening Day. Opening day was just me and Dad.

I sadly flashed backed to the last Opening Day. It was the last in many ways- the last one at Shea, the last one with Dad. We met the group beforehand, two and half hours before the game, when the gates opened. We toured the stadium, remembering our favorite Opening Day memories. After lunch of Nathan's hot dogs and fries, we separated and went to our seats. Dad and I were amazed at the new stadium looming beyond the walls in centerfield. We laughed as he recounted how he and his dad had to sit on freshly painted seats during Shea's inaugural Opening Day. I had heard that story every year but in 2008 it was better.

As I watched the clips of the crowds marveling at the new stadium, I wondered if Judy, Billy, Joan, and Vinny were there. I wondered if they'd miss me on Saturday.

LILY

Thursday   April 16, 2009

It must have been a special night. Another anniversary that I was somehow a part of but didn't remember. I held back asking.

We were eating in the dining room. Another romantically set table. One thing Craig didn't have on his profile (or at least Annie didn't mention it) was that he was a good cook. Even before I had resigned myself to my fate, I looked forward to his meals. Tonight it was Chinese food.

As I bit into the egg roll, I asked "Did you make this?"

"I could tell you yes but you might notice the take out boxes. I did make the stir fry, though."

"Sounds good." And it was, at first.

Halfway through dinner, sweat started to bead on my forehead. I felt queasy. I looked down at the stir fry. I thought it was chicken and mixed vegetables. I had taken two mouthfuls and loved it. "Craig, what is this?"

"It's stir fry."

"Yeah, I know but what's in it?"

My stomach started to flip and I knew I was going to be sick.

"Chicken and mixed vegetables. Don't you like it?"

I nodded my head yes because I did like it.

"Craig, what was in the egg rolls?"

"I don't know. I told you I didn't make them. Why? You liked them. You ate all of it."

"Was there fish in them?"

"Yes, there was a little shrimp in them. Why?" He looked at my quizzically.

"Oh my god, Craig. I'm allergic to fish." One thing about me he clearly didn't know.

I got up and ran for the bathroom in the kitchen. I slowed to a fast walk when I got through the dining room door into the foyer. I held onto the walls. The world had started to blacken at the edges.

I heard him get up and run after me. "Wait, Lillian." There was no time to wait.

I was a few feet from the bathroom when he grabbed me. He couldn't think I was trying to escape.

I grabbed for the wall to stabilize myself while the world swam around me. I fell to the floor. My eyes were closed. I rolled over onto to my back. "Craig, I really have to use the bathroom. I don't feel well."

I opened my eyes. Craig was straddled over me. Laude was circling us, barking and jumping for his arm. I saw a glint of light off something silver and thin. It was coming towards me. I panicked. I struggled to get away. I tried to push his arms away. One arm was holding me down. The other one was aiming for my left arm. I felt a piercing in my left arm. He let go of me, a smile on his face.

"What the fuck was that?," I screamed. I had originally thought it was a knife coming at me. It had been a needle. I had no idea what he had injected me with. I didn't wait for an answer. He had let go of me and I got up and ran to the bathroom. Laude was on my heels.

My heart was pounding. The shock of learning I ate seafood, the shock of being injected with something and the fear of what it was had elevated my pulse.

I finished in the bathroom. I knew it was only a matter of time before I would be sick again. I left the bathroom. My head and heart were pounding.

Craig was seated on one of the stools at the kitchen. His head was in his hands.

"Craig, I need to go back downstairs. I'm not feeling well."

"Audrey would never have said that."

I wasn't sure if he was talking to me or to himself.

"I don't know what you injected me with. I really don't feel well and I'm going to go downstairs."

He looked at me, his eyes blazing. This was it. The moment he would snap. For weeks, I had worried about it.

Incredulously, he said, "I was trying to help you. You said you were allergic to seafood." He looked away, talking to himself. "Audrey would never have used language like that."

"I'm guessing you never tried to kill Audrey." I was aggravated, I didn't feel well and I shouldn't have said it.

He was up, throwing me against the wall before I even registered him getting off the stool. He roared "No!" I saw the look I hadn't seen since the first night I had met him. The look that revealed the derangement that lay beneath the handsome exterior. He kept me pinned against the wall. "I would never hurt Audrey. I loved Audrey. And how could you think I'd hurt my own mother! It was an accident. If I had just put up that carbon monoxide alarm like she told me they'd still be here. How could you say that?," he yelled. At a lower volume, he continued, "I was trying to help you. That's all I have ever wanted to do."

"Craig, I really don't feel well." I was lightheaded. My stomach was starting to churn again. I wasn't sure what I needed more, to lie down or to get to the bathroom again. I felt worse than I had ever felt before after ingesting seafood. I was starting to worry more about what he had injected me with. "What did you inject me with?"

"It was epinephrine to stop the anaphylactic shock. You said you were allergic." He kept me pinned against the wall but with less force. The crazed look was gone, for now, replaced with one of genuine concern.

"I wasn't going to into anaphylactic shock. I was going to be sick." I tried not to panic about the possible side effects of epinephrine. At best, I would have an elevated pulse and blood pressure for a while. At worst, the elevated blood pressure would cause a stroke.

Very seriously, he looked at me. "That's a food intolerance. Not a food allergy. Really, Lillian, you should have said that." He had switched off his anger as quickly as he had switched it on. He lowered me to the floor, let go of my arms and stepped away.

"Craig, I need to lie down."

"Ok, let me get you downstairs." He lightly touched my arm. He looked horrified when I flinched.

Returning to my bedroom, I lay down, concentrating on my breathing, hoping to slow down my pulse and blood pressure. A few minutes later I was back in the bathroom getting rid of more of the dinner. Afterwards, I lay back down and rethought the evening.

In the seconds it took for him to throw me against the wall, the spell was broken.

It took me two days to recover. Two days to wonder how long ago Audrey and his mother had died from carbon monoxie poisoning, from what he had thought was his negligence. There was something about me that had reminded him of Audrey. But when I had cursed at him, the reminder was gone. I was desperate to get out of here before he saw more he didn't like.

I didn't have time to devise a new plan to escape. The plan came to me.

NATHAN

Saturday 12 p.m. April 18, 2009

I wasn't sure why I was going. Annie had mentioned how Lily had gone to Mets games with her father as long as she could remember. Lily had kept going every Saturday home game even after he had died. Annie had said she sounded depressed after each one since his death, but joked maybe it was because of the way the season had played out. I thought maybe it was the evil Phillies fan in Annie that had made the joke.

She had thought since Lily hadn't mentioned it she hadn't renewed for the season. Annie had assumed Lily had let the plan end with her father and with Shea Stadium. I was surprised when in March the tickets arrived. I had put them with the rest of the mail that had been collecting.

When I woke up in the morning, I decided I should go. I had already talked to everyone else in Lily's life. According to Annie, these people had known her since she could walk. I had run out of ideas to find her.

I filed through security with the rest of the masses and climbed the flights of stairs to the 500 level. I missed Shea's ramps and wondered if Lily would too. I wandered the walkways until I found section 523 and climbed to row 14. I was surprised that thirty minutes before the game how crowded the stadium was. I eased past the four filled seats and sat in seat five. As I settled in my seat, I looked to my right to see the four faces staring at me.

The two women had tears in their eyes and the two men looked at me curiously. "Who are you?," asked the man next to me.

Before I could answer, the thin sixty something year old woman next to him interjected. "Billy, that's not polite. Hi, I'm Judy. This is Billy, Joan and Vinny. We've been sitting together for over 20 years." Vinny was on the end, Joan in between Judy and Vinny. They all looked to be in their sixties.

"Hi. I'm Nathan. I guess you're Lillian's friends."

They all smiled and answered in unison. "Yep, we're 'The Saturday-ers'" and all laughed. I smiled with them. It was an old joke that they had obviously told many times.

Joan had stopped laughing first. "Oh good. We were afraid Lillian had changed her mind. Will she be here next week?"

Judy spoke next, "We know she had a hard time last year. How is she?"

I didn't want to tell them. I saw a beer vendor and signaled him over. "Five, please."

I thought making friends was my best strategy and there's no better way to make friends than buying a round of beers.

After many thanks and a few toasts, all to the new stadium and to a successful season, I asked "How well do you know Lillian?"

Vinny answered first. "She's a sweet girl." His wife, Joan, elbowed him in the side. "Sorry, woman. We've sat with her and her dad over twenty years. We were worried the first day he showed up with her. We expected her to start to crying in the third, right?"

"The second," laughed Billy.

Vinny looked around at the others, who all nodded their heads.

Billy added, "We were shocked when he showed up the next week, too. I've never seen a child sit through games like that!"

"At the third Saturday, I lost ten dollars to Judy on that one. I never thought they'd be back," grinned Vinny.

"Easy money. Wouldn't get me much in this stadium, as our new friend Nathan has just learned." They all laughed. I just hoped the forty dollars in beer yielded some information. So far, not so good. "I knew they'd be back. Lillian was mesmerized."

Vinny added, "She could only say a few words when she first started coming. But 'Mets' was one of them."

"How old was she when Wally started to teach her to score?" Joan asked.

"Four maybe. I don't think she could spell her name yet." Billy answered. They all laughed again. I could picture them in Shea, all six of them cheering the Mets through a lot of laughs.

The national anthem started and question and answer time was over.

After the third inning, Judy got up to use the ladies' room. "I didn't want to say it with the wife here, don't want to upset her. I saw the shield when you showed your I.D. for the beer. What are you really doing here?"

Might as well tell the truth, "Looking for Lily."

"She in trouble?"

"Yes."

"I find that hard to believe. You sure you got the right girl?"

"I'm sorry. She's not in trouble with the law. She's missing."

"Oh my god!" He looked to his right to make sure Joan and Vinny didn't hear him. They were busy watching the t-shirt launch. Quieter, he asked, "How long?"

"Too long. I've run out of leads. This guy look familiar?" I showed him both pictures of Franco/Franklin.

"No, but last season she didn't talk too much. She still came to each game, kept score like her Daddy taught her. But she was pretty quiet. And those last games, as the Mets lost the division, we were all in shock." He looked away and appeared upset. Billy seemed to be thinking about Wally, Lily and the end of the Mets 2008 season. I wasn't sure what he was most upset by.

He passed the photos down to Joan and Vinny and asked, "You ever see this guy?"

They both looked carefully but answered no.

The inning started and we watched the lead off batter walk on four pitches. A few minutes later, we cheered as the Mets infield turned a great double play. As we saw Judy climbing the steps to our seats, Billy said "I'm sorry we can't be of more help." The conversation about Lily was over.

At the end of the game, they all said good bye and asked me to give my regards to Lillian. Except Billy, who just said "Good luck."

I didn't learn anything new that was going to help. But I was glad I had come. I felt closer to Lily. And the Mets won.

LILY

Saturday   April 18, 2009

Lying on the bed, I watched the Mets game. I was feeling better, but tired. The effects of the epinephrine only lasted a few hours but the effects of the dinner lasted much longer. I was dehydrated from the food 'intolerance' and terrified by Craig's reaction. He came down more times than usual that night to ask if I was alright. He got one word responses to his questions.

"Are you alright?"

"Yes."

"Do you need anything?"

"No."

Then I would hear him lock the door and slowly go up the stairs. He took Laude out as scheduled but the door remained locked. We both knew things were different. My days of relative freedom were over.

I watched the Mets pre-game show sourly. It was the first Saturday game of the season. I should be there. It would have been the first time I would see the new stadium in person. Would Joan, Billy, Judy and Vinny miss me? And if they did, what would they do? If Annie hadn't done anything to find me, surely a group I only saw 13 times a year wouldn't do anything meaningful.

It was a good game and the Mets won. I had heard Craig's car leave before first pitch and return sometime during the middle of the game. I didn't think anything of it until after he took Laude out that night. After she returned, I got up to brush my teeth and get ready for bed. I found a white envelope, with the Mets emblem on it, by the door.

"I'm sorry" was written across it. I opened it to find two Mets tickets for next Saturday. I was finally getting out.

LILY

8 a.m.   Saturday   April 25, 2009

I woke to the sound of the doggie door unlocking and something being dropped in. Craig had said he'd take me to the Mets game but I found that hard to believe. But, there at the door was a Mets t-shirt and jacket. I picked them up and a box dropped out. I looked at it quizzically. It was a box of hair color.

His voice boomed from the speaker. "That's the only way we're going. Pick you up at eleven."

The only way I was going was as a red-head.

Ever punctual, Craig knocked on the bedroom door at eleven.

I had been pacing the last twenty minutes. I was finally getting out of this house but knew freedom would not be as easy as it appeared. "I'm ready," I told him.

He opened the door and tried, unsuccessfully, to not look shocked at my appearance. It had taken me an hour to color my hair- twenty minutes to read the directions, twenty minutes to apply it, ten minutes on, and ten minutes to rinse out and style. This didn't include the following ten minutes spent staring in the mirror. The 'amber' color described was more copper.

"I'm ready, too." I headed up the stairs, knowing Laude would follow. I turned when I heard Craig.

"Sorry, Laude. You can't come today."

"What?," I asked. "She hasn't left my side in months. Can't she come with us?"

"You didn't really think she could come, did you?," he replied.

"Why not? Maybe it's dog day at Shea. I mean, Citi Field."

"It's not."

"What's the weather like? Maybe she can wait in the car."

"No, she can't. Let's go." I remained on the step as he closed the bedroom and Laude started whimpering. Tears welled in my eyes. Craig turned to go up the stairs and we were almost eye to eye.

"If you don't want to go, we don't have to," he said. The sarcasm hung in the air.

I turned and walked up the stairs.

We both knew why Laude was staying- collateral.

We were walking down the crowded concourse when I said, "Craig, I have to go to the bathroom."

"Ok, fine." He looked from side to side, his hand never leaving my arm.

I stopped, "There's a ladies' room, there."

Craig grabbed my arm harder and directed me to the family bathroom. He started to come in with me. "What are you doing? You can't go in the bathroom with me."

His grip tightened more on my arm, to the point of pain. "Fine, I'll wait out here. Don't forget what I told you."

As the door closed, I thought 'How could I?'"

I had gotten in the car planning to closely watch the route so I could tell the police how to get here. As I belted in, he placed a blindfold on me, then sunglasses. All I would be able to describe to the police was what the house looked like. I never saw a house number and I still had no idea what town I was in or even if I was still on Long Island.

What seemed like an hour later, I felt the car slow. Craig pulled off the sunglasses and blindfold. I squinted as the bright sun hit my eyes. I recognized where I was once I could see. We were getting off the highway and heading for the main parking lot.

Before I could signal one of the many police officers directing traffic, Craig grabbed my arm and said "If you ever want to see Laude again, you will remain quiet." Before I could say anything, he added. "They'll never find her. She'll die of starvation, whimpering for you."

The deranged look was back. The man I was scared of was back. The crazy eyes were back. How could I have ever seen anything else?

He knew he had made his point when he saw the tears in my eyes.

Craig directed me to our seats. He sat in the aisle seat. Despite the large crowd, there were plenty of empty seats around us. I watched from the outfield as the Mets starting pitcher, Mike Pelfrey, took his last warm up pitches, praying someone would sit next to me.

Craig hadn't let go of my arm since leaving the bathroom. He tightened his grip when he caught me looking at the empty seat. "Don't worry. No one's going to be sitting next to you."

He smiled. A smile a week ago that I had found attractive was now frightening.

I knew I had to get away but couldn't sacrifice Laude to do so. She was all I had left of my parents. I prayed for a long game to give me time.

The Mets were keeping up their side of the bargain, by scoring three in the first and Pelfrey did his usual to keep the pace slow by pitching into deep counts. With the bases loaded in the Mets half of the third, I thought I had my way. Our section, now full except for the seat next to me, all on their feet as Carlos Beltran's fly to left looked as if it was headed to us. Everyone was cheering, anticipating a grand slam, even Craig. If I could run to the car and get the GPS, I'd know where Laude was. Craig would expect me to run to security, not the car. I just needed a head start. I started to my right.

No one heard my yell, as Craig grabbed my arm, over the moan of the crowd as the left fielder caught the ball on the warning track and ended the inning.

"Don't forget how fast I am, Lillian." he whispered into my ear. "I will beat you to the car."

I cringed realizing he knew me very well. He knew I wouldn't run to save myself but to save Laude.

He shook his head. "I love you but my patience is wearing thin that it's not returned."

I sat still for the next inning, Craig's firm grasp on my forearm pinning me to the armrest.

I had no options. If I ran, he'd catch me, like he did every other time. If I screamed, he'd convince them there was something wrong with me. I'd taken a good look at myself in the bathroom mirror. The unnaturally bright red hair only drew attention to my sallow skin. The dark rings under my eyes were accentuated by my thin face. I wasn't sure how much weight I had lost. Between the two of us, he looked like the sane one, the stable one. If questioned, he'd turn on that charm and convince them everything was fine.

I didn't make eye contact with anyone. I would sit quietly the rest of the game. My only chance was to cause a scene at the car. I was debating how to do this when the woman behind me started poking me in the shoulder.

"Look! It's you! Look!," she yelled. Part of me expected to see my picture on the scoreboard with "Have you seen her?" posted with it. No part of me expected to see the Kiss Cam.

She kept tapping me on the shoulder, "Kiss! Kiss!"

I turned to find Craig smiling and starting to lean in. I instinctively pulled away.

"What you don't want our first kiss broadcasted in front of 40,000?," he whispered. Boos started because of the lack of a kiss. As if I hadn't had a bad enough two months, I was now being booed in my home ballpark. He kissed me on the top of my head and the boos stopped.

I caught a glimpse of us before they went on to a more willing couple and knew 40,000 people thought I was the crazy one. Any woman dodging a kiss from such a handsome man had to be insane.

I overheard the woman behind me talking about us. "She's so shy. Maybe it's their first date."

"Oh, if she only knew," Craig whispered.

"Let's go," Craig said while pulling me out of my seat in the middle of the seventh inning.

"What?" I'd never left a game early.

He didn't say it again and started pushing me up the stairs. Many were headed the same way.

"Craig, it's the seventh inning." I needed more time.

Craig became impatient with the crowd and shoved past a couple. I looked desperately around. If we left early, the parking lot wouldn't be crowded enough to cause a commotion.

At the top of the stairs, I headed to the left, knowing that was the quickest route to the car. Craig headed to the right, the way we had come, through the crowded food court.

A section over, I saw a man frantically looking around, as if he had lost his child. He saw me looking at him and his frenzied motions stopped. He couldn't take his eyes off me. If I wasn't already with Craig, I'd be concerned about his intent glare.

Before I looked away, he put his index finger to his lips, motioning me to be quiet. I looked from the stranger to Craig and back. I wasn't sure who I was more afraid of. I watched in disbelief as he continued to come my way. He never looked away from me. I looked at Craig. He didn't seem to notice the stranger.

As the crowd thinned, Craig looked back to me and pulled me closer. He followed my line of sight.

Craig jerked me away from staring at the strange man, who was still watching me intently and now only twenty feet away.

"Lily!," I thought I heard the stranger scream as Craig pulled me further into the concourse.

He started running at me. But Craig ran faster.

NATHAN

12:45pm

Again, I didn't know why I was at Citi Field. "The Saturday-ers" were nice but not helpful. It was unlikely that Franco had stalked Lily that long.

Instead of going to my, I mean Lily's, seat, I walked the concourse watching the fans checking out the new stadium - the numerous food stands, stores and Shea Stadium tributes. I stood on the bridge beyond right centerfield, watching people lining up to take pictures with the old home run apple below. I looked down at my soda and decided I needed something stronger. Heading to a beer stand, I stopped. I saw a tall man, with an athletic build, standing outside the family bathroom. He stood out because of his on guard stance and his lack of orange and blue attire. I looked down at myself and noted I wasn't dressed in Mets paraphanelia either.

The blond man's eyes darted back and forth. He saw me watching him and turned to the bathroom door and knocked on it furiously. No one else took notice of his strange behavior. The door openend and a small red-headed woman came out. I shook my head wondering why she'd choose such a terrible, unnatural color.

He grabbed her arm and swung her around, away from me. I could only see her flaming red hair. I debated following them but knew if she was in trouble there were plenty of police to ask for help from.

I watched them for a few feet but then lost them in the crowd.

◇

My eyes were glazing over at the slow pace of the game. I had finished my beer and was debating getting another when Vinny elbowed me in the side.

"That date looks like its going badly," Vinny said.

"What?" I couldn't hear him over the booing. I looked to the field, the Nationals players were running out on the field to take their places. "What's with all the booing?"

He nudged me and pointed to the screen in centerfield. The Kiss Cam was up on the screen framing a couple - an eager man and terrified woman. Boos intensified as I watched her profile. She was leaning back to evade his kiss. She turned away from him, inadvertently looking directly at the camera.

"Oh shit! That's Lily!," I yelled. I got up to run to her but didn't know where to go.

"Vinny, where is that?"

The cameraman went to a different couple, who were met with cheers when they kissed. Vinny didn't hear me over the cheers.

"Vinny, that last couple, where was that?" I asked again.

"I don't know," he shrugged. "All the seats are the same here. Who can tell?" He rambled on about the different colored seats at Shea and how each level at Citi had the same green seats. I ran off to find an employee before I heard more about the orange, blue, green and red seats of Shea again.

"Camera room? Where's the camera room?" I yelled at the first employee I could find. He stared back at me blankly.

I ran and found a fellow cop, flashing my badge. "Miccoli, 1-0-9. I need to find the..." I stuttered not knowing where I needed to go, knowing my time was limited. "wherever they control the scoreboard. There was a kidnapped woman on the screen during the Kiss Cam. I need to find out where they're sitting."

He directed me to the productions room, one level down. I held out my badge to anyone who tried to get in my way. I slammed it against the large window, looking into the production room and banged on the glass until they let me in. The employees were watching several televisions, showing the multiple views of the stadium. Lily wasn't on any of them.

They let me in and I scanned the monitors more closely. My screams for the "The red-headed girl. Where was she sitting?" was met with blank stares. "The Kiss-Cam. The girl who wouldn't kiss the man."

That registered with them. "Brutal right?," said one of them.

I slammed my fist down. "Just tell me where she is!"

Startled by my outburst, they returned to their monitors. They scrolled through video and talked to the cameraman as I paced the small room. "Field Level. Section 138."

I started to run to her but stopped, realizing I didn't know which way to go. I turned and the employee anticipated my question. "To the left of the apple." he yelled, pointing to the outfield.

I ran out of the room, back to the stairs, down to the Field level.

I looked desperately around as I got to the field level for the section signs. I ran to the left, towards the outfield and saw the section signs counting up, "118, 119..." I was frantically scanning the crowd as I stood under the section sign "138" when I saw her. She was approaching the top of the stairs, twenty feet to my left, being pulled up the stairs by Franco.

We locked eyes and I smiled. I'd finally found her. I put my index finger to my lips, urging her to remain quiet. Franco hadn't seen me and I needed it to stay that way until I was close enough to grab him. Her beautiful green eyes bulged with fear. I regretted not pulling out my badge to prove I was help.

She held her ground, looking at me shocked, as he pulled her in the opposite direction. Franco surveyed the area and saw me.

"Lily!," I yelled.

I watched as she struggled to get away. Without slowing, Franco picked her up, holding her against his side, and ran. She kicked in protest, to no avail.

The crowd was thick, and getting thicker as the throngs headed into the concourse as "Take Me Out To The Ballgame" began to play. I struggled to keep up, between Franco's speed and the crowd growing larger in the food court, lining up to get a beer before they stopped selling.

"Stop! Police," I yelled but no one heard me over the music and crowd noise. "Stop!" I yelled again.

My frequent walks around the stadium oriented me to its several exits. Franco/Franklin had already missed one and was running past a second. I knew I'd pass fellow police officers before he got to the third, the main entry, the Jackie Robinson Rotunda. They could radio ahead to stop his exit.

As he crossed the bridge, he looked to his left and noticed the Bullpen exit, one flight below. I was approaching the bridge when he darted to the left and down the staircase to the exit.

I ran down the parallel staircase, a quicker way to the exit had he noticed it before the bridge, and was neck and neck with them. I saw officers manning the exit and yelled for them to stop Franco, flashing my badge. He was no longer carrying Lily on his side. She was back on her feet, being dragged towards the exit by him. He had slowed when he saw the police and smiled. Hoping to distract the officers, he pointed to someone else then sprinted towards the turnstiles but was stopped by one of the officers.

Lily looked around frantically as the other officer grabbed her.

LILY

"Lily?" he asked.

I couldn't have possibly heard him right. I'd never seen him before. He didn't look familiar at all. And no one calls me that, except Annie and Dad. But it didn't matter if I knew him, he knew me.

NATHAN

After months of searching, I had found her. I swiped the bright red hair out of her eyes.

"Who the hell are you? Lillian! Who is this?" her abductor/Franco/Franklin/whoever the hell he was yelled.

She shook her head. "I don't know," she answered.

LILY

Before I could say anything else, the stranger had arrested Craig. In shock, I heard him turn to me and ask "Where's Laude?"

"I don't know. I don't know where he's been keeping us. It took us under an hour to get here but I was blindfolded. He could have been driving around aimlessly for all I know. But I can bring you to his car. He's got a GPS."

"Take me to his car." Officers escorted Craig away in handcuffs while he screamed and struggled. "Lillian, don't do this. I love you. Tell these men it's all a mistake. We're getting married. We're together. You picked me. What are these guys talking about kidnapping? There was no kidnapping." The further he got away, the louder he shouted. I tried not to notice the people staring from the bridge above.

I took the man to the car and he directed an officer to take me to the precinct to wait.

I waited at the precinct for what seemed like forever. I fidgeted in the uncomfortable hard chair and drummed my fingers on the desk. After giving my statement, the officer had left me at his desk, never giving me any updates.

If the GPS didn't have 'home' listed, surely the officers could figure out his address. It just seemed to be taking so long.

I closed my eyes hoping that time would go faster if I wasn't watching the clock. I didn't know how long my eyes were closed when I heard "I'm sorry" and I thought the worst. I opened my eyes and there she was. Tail wagging, tongue licking my face. The last ten weeks were over.

I jumped up and grabbed her from him, holding Laude tight as she squirmed.

"I'm sorry this took so long. Lot of traffic out there. I'm sure you were worried. She's even cuter than I thought she'd be." Another odd statement from this stranger.

"I'm Miccoli. I mean....Nathan." He seemed nervous. "I'm sorry I should have introduced myself earlier. I was just so shocked to find you. And I wanted to get Laude as soon as possible. I can't tell you how happy I am to see you. You gave your statement right? We'll have to call Annie."

Instead of shaking my hand like I expected a police officer to do, he gave me the biggest bear hug I had ever had, lifting me off my feet. He certainly was happy to see me.

Nathan placed me back down and motioned for me to sit, while he sat at the desk.

"We learned a lot about him in just a few hours and seemed to have pieced most of it together. We're waiting for his statement to confirm it. It all makes a sense now. He has a history of mental illness. Institutionalized after his father died when he was seventeen. His wife and mother died last year."

"Carbon monoxide poisoning."

"Yes," he said. He looked at me closely. "How'd you know?"

"He put up a carbon monoxide monitor in my apartment. He made a huge deal of it when he told me. Was his wife's name Audrey?"

"Yes, how'd you know that?"

"He called me it once but covered up real fast. Another time he told me I wasn't like Audrey. In the moment, he wasn't happy about it."

"So you know he was Tony's assistant?"

"I learned it along the way. I had a lot of time to put things together." I looked at my hands. "Too long," I added.

"Me too," he said.

I couldn't believe I had been kept in a basement for ten weeks. Thankfully, Nathan interrupted my trip down memory lane. "We found pictures in his home, on the second floor. You look a lot like her. Before the red hair of course."

"Oh my god, I forgot! The box said it would wash out in a few washings." I took a few strands in my fingers and marveled at the red color.

"At least now we know why you."

"What? A girl whose online profile received only one response isn't likely to be stalked and kidnapped. Is she?" I feinted being insulted.

"No, no. Annie said you'd say something silly about this."

"I doubt that's the first thing she said about me." I grinned as I said it fully knowing that Annie must have told Nathan Miccoli a lot about me.

NATHAN

I thought back to my first meeting with Annie. The first thing Annie told me about Lily was that she didn't know what she would do without her. I didn't think that was what Lily expected.

"And what do you think was the first thing Annie said about you?," I asked.

"The first thing she told *you* was that I was single." She smiled at me and those green eyes sparkled. She was just how I had pictured all these weeks.

It wasn't the first thing Annie told me, but she had definitely mentioned it.

LILY

3:56 p.m.

After we stopped smiling at each other, Nathan told me it was time to go home. My home.

"Officer Rinso will take you home. I'll stop by later if you're not too tired." He paused, debating what to say. "For a few follow up questions." Nathan directed me to Office Rinso who was waiting in the lobby.

I started to say good bye when I realized I had a problem. "That would be great but I don't have keys."

"Of course, hold on." He turned around and went back to the desk for his jacket. After fiddling with a keychain, he came back, handing me keys. "Here you go." I looked at them expecting to see my Mets and schnauzer keychains, assuming they had found my purse at Craig's. But they were the set I gave Annie after we changed the locks. Why would he have these on his keychain?

"Thanks, one more question," I said.

"Yes, the Mets won."

For a complete stranger, he seemed to know me pretty well.

NATHAN

7:00 p.m.

I debated whether or not to tell her. She should know. But I didn't want to ruin her first day home. But, she should know. There was no sense waiting. I didn't have keys anymore so I rang the bell. I heard Laude barking and running back and forth.

"Coming," she yelled. She must have been on the patio. I'm sure she'd be avoiding the bedroom for awhile.

I heard Lily open the peep hole and then open the door.

"Hi, could I come in?" I was anxious to get this over. I was also anxious to learn of her reaction to my living in her apartment while she was gone.

She smiled and answered. "The man that saved me from crazy eyes- definitely."

"Crazy eyes. I didn't know what you had meant when you told Annie that but I do now." Craig had indeed been crazed when I got to the precinct after getting Laude. After hours in the holding cell, he definitely had "crazy eyes".

Lily directed me into the living room. "I'd offer you something to eat or drink but nothing could be good after being gone ten weeks. I'm afraid to even open the refrigerator!"

"I think you'll find everything in good condition."

A puzzled look was the only response. I guess Annie hadn't mentioned I'd stayed a little bit while she was gone. Best to bring that up later.

"I have something difficult to tell you. I thought about not telling you but thought you should know. There's no easy way to say this." I paused. Partially to stay off the task of telling her, partially to stay off the pain I expected to cause her. I took a deep breath and said it as quickly as I could.

"Charlie killed your parents."

All afternoon I had pictured her possible responses. Shock, disbelief, tears, anger. But that's not what I got. And I didn't know what to make of it.

"Uh, well...that makes me feel better," she said.

LILY

From his horrified look, my response was unexpected.

"I guess I should explain that."

"Probably." He was definitely puzzled but I could see he was saving judgment.

"I could really use a beer though. It's been a rough day."

"Sure, I'll get us some." Instead of walking to the door to leave to go buy beer, he walked to the refrigerator. I had just told him I was afraid to open the refrigerator. The milk and anything else I had in there was disgusting to think about. He opened it, grabbed something - two Sam Adams Summer Ale beers. Mouth open, I stared at him. How the hell did that get in there and how did he know that was in there?

After noticing my shock, he gave a sheepish grin. The tables were turned. "Maybe I should explain that," he said.

With a raised eyebrow, I replied "Yes, probably."

"Annie gave me your keys. I started staying here on my off days. Then I started to stay most nights. I know I shouldn't have, but Annie said it was alright. I liked being here. She thought I would find something useful."

"Did you?"

"I did. A few things. After Ms. June told me Franklin's picture was the superintendent's assistant, Franco, especially."

I knew he was thinking about the same thing I was, the cameras.

"I know he had cameras in here. I figured it out. And he told me. He was proud of them. How I never suspected. How he learned so much about me and Laude. He swears there were none in the bathroom, here or at his place. It was horrifying."

"Someone stalking you, re-creating your bedroom is horrifying. That room he kept you in was creepy."

I giggled at that. "Are you saying my bedroom is creepy?" I could barely get out the statement I was laughing so hard.

NATHAN

Telling a woman her bedroom was creepy was not a smooth move. "But the one here is really nice!" I said trying to save myself. I'm not sure if that made things better or worse. Telling a woman I had just met that I liked her bedroom, that I'd slept there many nights, was also not a smooth move.

She just shook her head and motioned for me to follow her out onto the patio. I sat in the chair next to her and Laude jumped on her lap. We both looked out at the ocean.

"I missed this. The smell of the ocean, the cool breeze on my face, the randomness of the waves, the planes flying regularly overhead."

We sat there, enjoying the sunset and the waves, slowly sipping on our beers.

"So, pretty odd that I was glad to hear about Charlie."

"I'm sure you can explain."

"Is he in jail?"

"No, and I can't make a case to get him there. I'm sorry. But the way he's been living, he'll end up there sooner or later."

"For months, I've wondered why Aunt Florence had stopped talking to me. We were always very close. She was like a second mom. Her home a second home. After my parents were killed, she didn't comfort me, barely spoke to me. She gave me this place and walked out. At least I know why now."

LILY

7:30 a.m.   Sunday   May 3, 2009

"So, what's for breakfast?" Annie asked as I answered the phone.

"Bagel and cream cheese," I answered.

"Oh," she said surprised, "no bakery?"

I didn't want to tell her Laude and I had stood outside Rein's for five minutes as I debated going in. I wasn't sure if I didn't go in because of memories of Craig or of Aunt Florence. I decided to go to the bagel store again, because maybe we had started a new tradition last Sunday.

"No bakery. Bagel and cream cheese sounded good," I told her.

"It does. Have you talked to Olivia?"

"Yep. All set to start work in Virginia on May 18."

There was a pause while she debated whether to ask. "So, have you seen Nathan?"

"Yes," I answered.

"He sure spent a lot of time at your place and a lot of time looking for you."

"Uh-uh."

"He's a nice guy," she said.

"He is," I agreed. Then she started talking about Harry.

At least one good thing had come out of my disappearance. I got my best friend back.

LILY

Sunday   May 9, 2009

Not surprisingly, the sound of the ocean was no longer soothing. But, watching the rhythmic crashing of the waves still was. I could sit here for hours just watching it, Laude on my lap, hoping none of the Long Beach police officers came by and gave me a ticket. I felt a tap on my shoulder and jumped in surprise.

"Sorry, I didn't mean to startle you. You're pretty zoned in."

I took the iPod earbuds out and the classical music could still be heard.

I couldn't help but smile as I looked up at Nathan. "Hi, Nathan. How are you?"

"Good, thanks. You?"

"Making it." He sat down next to me on the boardwalk's bench and Laude jumped into his arms.

"I went to your place. Looks like the open house is a success."

"Hope so. I'm leaving next week. You interested?"

I got a puzzled look back from that question. I figured he might want to buy the condo since he came to the open house, since he had lived there for a bit. Lord knows, I would give him a good deal.

"Not in the apartment, no," he said as he smiled and looked out at the ocean.

It seemed like an odd response. What else could he be interested in? Then, I heard Annie's voice in my head "You, silly." And I smiled, the first true smile in a long time.

Made in the USA
Charleston, SC
30 June 2015